"Neither of you has any idea what Mrs. Gallagher wanted to see Mrs. Donovan about this morning?"

"I'm afraid not," I answered. Rose shook her head.

"Then I guess I'll be going." Detective Sturgill braced his hands on his knees and pushed himself to his feet. "Mrs. Donovan, I'm sorry for the loss of your friend."

"Thank you."

"I'll show the detective out," I told her.

He and I walked to the door together. When Sturgilll stepped out onto the porch, I followed him.

"There's something you weren't saying in there," I said. "How did Mrs. Gallagher actually die?"

"Like I said, she had a fall."

"But you don't think it was an accident."

"Ms. Travis, you have a suspicious mind."

"So do you," I replied. "And I'm guessing something's bugging you about how the fall happened. Or else you wouldn't be asking questions . . ."

Books by Laurien Berenson

Melanie Travis Mysteries

A PEDIGREE TO DIE FOR
UNDERDOG
DOG EAT DOG
HAIR OF THE DOG
WATCHDOG
HUSH PUPPY
UNLEASHED
ONCE BITTEN
HOT DOG
BEST IN SHOW
JINGLE BELL BARK
RAINING CATS AND DOGS
CHOW DOWN
HOUNDED TO DEATH
DOGGIE DAY CARE MURDER
GONE WITH THE WOOF
DEATH OF A DOG WHISPERER
THE BARK BEFORE CHRISTMAS
LIVE AND LET GROWL
MURDER AT THE PUPPY FEST
WAGGING THROUGH THE SNOW
RUFF JUSTICE
BITE CLUB
HERE COMES SANTA PAWS
GAME OF DOG BONES
HOWLOWEEN MURDER
PUP FICTION
SHOW ME THE BUNNY
KILLER CUPID

A Senior Sleuths Mystery

PEG AND ROSE SOLVE A MURDER

Published by Kensington Publishing Corp.

Show Me
the Bunny

LAURIEN
BERENSON

Kensington Publishing Corp.
www.kensingtonbooks.com

KENSINGTON BOOKS are published by

Kensington Publishing Corp.
119 West 40th Street
New York, NY 10018

First Hardcover Edition: February 2022

First Mass Market Printing: March 2023
ISBN: 978-1-4967-3582-9

ISBN: 978-1-4967-3383-6 (ebook)

10 9 8 7 6 5 4 3 2 1

Printed in the United States of America

Chapter
One

"Aunt Rose! What are you doing here?"

I stood in the open doorway and stared in surprise at Rose Donovan—formerly known as Sister Anne Marie, of the Convent of Divine Mercy. It was late March and the first day of spring break. My husband, Sam, and our sons, Davey and Kevin, were all out of the house for the morning, so I'd been enjoying a rare moment of peace.

I hadn't been expecting any visitors—least of all this one.

Rose regarded me calmly across the front step. As always, her gaze was direct and composed, a vestige of the religious vocation that had occupied the majority of her life. Even a decade after she'd left the order, Rose still retained the upright posture and unruffled demeanor that had become second nature during her time in the convent.

"Where else would I be?" she inquired crisply.

"I don't know." I still felt as though I'd been caught off guard. "Nairobi? Guatemala? Appalachia? Last I heard, you and your husband, Peter, were off doing missionary work . . . um . . . somewhere."

"Then I can see we have some catching up to do."

Rose's lips pursed, a small sign of displeasure. For a woman in her sixties, her face was remarkably unlined. Short gray hair was anchored behind her ears. Tiny silver hoops hung from her lobes. They appeared to be her only nod to vanity. She didn't even have on a dab of lipstick.

"Aren't you going to invite me inside?" Rose asked.

"Yes, of course."

I would have already stepped back out of her way. Except that the six dogs crowded around the hallway behind me would have taken that as an invitation. They'd have gone scrambling through the open doorway to greet our guest— whether she wanted to meet them or not.

And in this case, I was pretty sure the answer to that was no.

"You'll have to deal with the dogs," I told her. Rose peered around me to survey the eager pack. "There appears to be a lot of them," she mentioned unnecessarily. "I will endeavor to manage."

Five of the dogs were Standard Poodles. Each one was big, black, and beautiful. The sixth dog was a small spotted mutt named Bud, who caused more commotion than all the Poodles put together. Stepping past me into the house, Rose lowered her hands and flapped them at the canine crew to chase them out of her way.

The Poodles recognized a dismissal when they saw one. They quickly fell back. Not Bud. He stood his ground and gazed up at Rose with adoring eyes. His stubby tail was wagging hard enough to make his whole hindquarter dance.

"What's the matter with that one?" Rose asked as she slipped off her light jacket and handed it to me. Bud's adorable greeting was clearly lost on her. "He doesn't seem to get it."

"Bud's a law unto himself." I took the coat and I stashed it in the closet. "Some idiots dumped him by the side of the road a couple of years ago and Davey and I brought him home. We're still working on civilizing him."

I smiled fondly at the little dog. Bud gave me a doggie grin in return. We both knew that civilizing idea was a joke. But, hey, at least he was housebroken.

Rose continued to gaze around the hallway with a critical eye. The Poodles might have retreated, but they hadn't gone far. Rose lifted a finger and pointed delicately. "That one could use some grooming. It looks like a bear."

"She," I corrected automatically.

The Poodle in question was a seven-month-old puppy who was growing out her coat for the show ring. We had been grooming her. But at this stage, she was supposed to resemble a big ball of fluff.

"She," Rose snapped. She was not amused.

"That's Plum—"

Her head turned my way. "Like the fruit?"

"Precisely."

"Why?"

I shrugged.

There was an answer to that question, but I knew Aunt Rose wouldn't like it. In a moment of whimsy, Sam had said that his new Poodle puppy was plum pretty. Then Davey had responded by calling her plum perfect. After we'd all had a good laugh, the name had stuck.

"Sam named her," I said instead. "She's his new puppy."

"Because for some reason you felt you needed another dog?"

We'd lost our elderly Poodle, Raven, in January. Sam had bred her, raised her, and shown her to her championship. The bitch's death from the infirmities of old age had come as a wrench. Plum wasn't here to replace Raven—we all loved the puppy for her own merits. But under the circumstances, it was nice for Sam to have a new Standard Poodle to weave his next set of dog show dreams around.

"Apparently so." I was determined that Rose wasn't going to succeed in putting me on the defensive before she'd even told me what she was doing here. I gestured toward the living room. With two boys and six dogs in the house, the big, bright space was filled with furniture that had been chosen for both comfort and durability. "Would you like to sit down?"

"Yes, I would." Rose strode into the middle of the room, then stopped. "If I take a seat on the couch, will a dog jump up on top of me?"

"Maybe." *No.*

But she didn't have to know that. There was something about my saintly Aunt Rose that always seemed to bring out my devilish side. It was probably a good thing that we didn't see each other often.

Rose glanced around the room, then picked the least comfortable chair there. It was sturdy, straight-backed, and had only a thin needle-point cushion covering its hard wooden seat. Sam had inherited that chair from an aging relative. Nobody ever sat in it. It was shoved in a corner against the wall.

Rose lifted the chair, carried it over, and set it down opposite the couch. In spite of myself, I was impressed. Rose was slender, but she had strength in those skinny arms.

"You," she said, gesturing toward the couch. "Sit."

If it came as a surprise that I wasn't the only one who obeyed her command, Rose didn't show it. I sank down on the middle cushion. Faith, dog of my heart, hopped up and snuggled close on one side of me. Faith's daughter, Eve, took the other side. The two male Poodles, Tar and Augie, sat down on the floor at either end of the couch like a Standard Poodle honor guard.

We all waited to see what Rose would do next.

"You and I have never gotten along, Melanie," she said. "Why is that?"

I swallowed heavily. That was a barbed question. And also one with too many answers to count.

Partly it was because our contact had been limited for the first three decades of my life. Rose had been a sister of Divine Mercy then. I'd attended the order's convent school, but once I'd graduated, there'd been little opportunity for us to interact with each other as adults. Or as equals.

I knew, however, that wasn't the only explanation for our prickly relationship. Through the years, I'd always felt as though Rose was comparing me—academically, spiritually, morally—to an unattainable standard, only to find me lacking. In her role as Sister Anne Marie, Rose had cast her earthly aspirations toward a Higher Authority. By contrast, my goals had always re-mained firmly grounded in the world around me that I could see and touch.

I had no intention of explaining all that to Rose, however. At best, she would be skeptical. At worst, laughingly dismissive. Neither response would bode well for the future of this conversation.

Now I'd let the silence linger for a few beats too long. Abruptly Rose frowned.

"Frankly, I blame Peg for our disunity," she announced.

Good answer, I thought. Better Aunt Peg than me. Because if my two aunts were inclined to brawl, I'd put my money on Peg every time.

Which was yet another reason why Rose and I were sitting here facing each other like adver-saries. My relatives have always been a conten-tious bunch. Family harmony was a fine idea, but it simply wasn't for us. In my family, some-one was always being asked to choose sides.

And when it came to the ongoing hostilities between Aunt Rose and Aunt Peg, I had chosen Peg. Deliberately. And repeatedly.

"Well," I said, "you know Aunt Peg. She marches to her own beat."

Rose snorted under her breath. "Peg is more likely to grab the drum and hit someone over the head with it."

"That too," I agreed mildly. When Rose didn't say anything else, I added, "Sam and Davey went to the hardware store to get supplies to fix the tree house. Kevin is at a playdate with a friend who lives up the street. We've probably got about an hour until mayhem descends. Maybe you'd like to use that time to tell me why you're here?"

"You've become very direct since the last time we saw each other. I like that." Rose peered at me across the low coffee table between us. "I'm here because I want you to help me with something."

"Sure," I replied without thinking. It was a bad habit of mine. "What do you need?"

"I'm hosting an Easter egg hunt, and I need someone to organize it for me. It occurred to me that you would be the perfect person for the job."

Me? I gulped. Maybe she was joking.

"Why me?" I asked.

"For one thing, it's spring break so you're free. Ten whole days, isn't it?" Rose smiled. "That seems like a generous amount of time."

Well, yes, it was. I worked half days as a special needs tutor at a private school in Greenwich, Connecticut. For the most part, the school catered to the needs of a very wealthy community. Students were held to a rigorous academic standard, and vacations were scheduled to allow ample time for their families to go skiing in Verbier or fly-fishing in Patagonia.

While my students were off jetting around

the world, however, I would be mostly sitting at home. Which still didn't mean that I wanted to devote my school holiday to hiding someone else's Easter eggs.

I curled my arm around Faith's neck and tangled my fingers in her tight curls. The big Poodle sighed happily and leaned her body into mine. I wanted to sigh too. I wished it wasn't too late to go back to the point in the conversation when Rose had merely been making fun of my dogs' names.

"You've always been good at solving mysteries," she plowed on. "So this should be right up your alley. Think of it as a mystery in reverse. Rather than searching for clues—or in this case, Easter eggs—you'll be the person hiding them. Imagine how satisfying that will be."

Honestly, it was hard for me to imagine anything about eggs that I would find satisfying—unless maybe they'd been scrambled in butter, topped with chives, and were served on a piece of French toast.

"Plus," Rose said, "everyone else was busy. Your brother and his family are taking a car trip to New Hampshire."

I knew that.

"I even tried to snag Claire. But her schedule was full too."

Claire was my ex-husband's wife, Davey's stepmother. She and Bob lived on the other side of

Stamford. Claire was an event planner and she was great at her job. Apparently she was also adept at sidestepping events she didn't want any part of. Too bad I didn't share that skill.

"And then," Rose finished triumphantly, "Peg volunteered you."

My gaze snapped upward from the depths of the couch. "When did you two start speaking again?"

"When Peter and I returned to the U.S. six weeks ago after our last posting came to an end. And you're wrong, we weren't in Guatemala, it was Honduras. Peg was kind enough to help us find a temporary place to stay."

Two thoughts immediately came to mind. One, Aunt Peg was never kind, and especially not when it came to her sister-in-law, Rose. And two, Rose and her husband had been back in the country for *six weeks*? How had that happened without my knowing about it?

Clearly, I did have some catching up to do.

"Surely you didn't ask Aunt Peg to help out with your Easter egg hunt?" The notion made me laugh.

"Of course not. Peg hasn't got a whimsical bone in her entire body. Besides, I'd be afraid she'd scare the poor children half to death. I asked Claire. She must have mentioned it to Peg, because Peg then called and said I should ask you. She told me you become boring when you don't have enough to do."

Me, *boring*? No way. Not ever.

I frowned and reconsidered. Well, possibly sometimes.

Abruptly I was struck by another thought. This one made me jump to my feet.

"Children," I said. "What children?"

Chapter Two

"I was getting to that," Aunt Rose said. "Perhaps you'd better sit down again."

"Children?" I repeated. "You and Peter have children? Like more than one? How did that happen?"

She motioned toward the couch behind me. Rose had that look on her face again: the Sister Anne Marie look. It was serene and self-assured, as if my compliance was assumed and she was merely waiting for me to get to it.

Which, of course, I did. Darn it. I hated being so predictable.

Faith had rolled into my spot on the cushion when I'd leapt up. Now she and Eve were squabbling over which of them was entitled to the extra space I'd unexpectedly provided. I used both hands to nudge the two Poodles out of my way so I could sit down again.

Rose waited until I was settled before she continued. "They are not Peter's and my children—"

"Thank God for that," I muttered. Ten minutes with Aunt Rose and already I was invoking the deity. If that wasn't a sign of trouble, I didn't know what was.

"If you keep interrupting, this will be a very long story."

I suspected it would be a long story regardless. We Turnbull women—myself included, Turnbull was my maiden name—weren't known for our brevity. We excelled in imagination, however. Which was why I was sure that the tale Rose was about to tell me would be a doozy.

"Peter and I have opened a women's shelter in Stamford," she began.

My eyes widened. Then the questions came pouring out. "When? Where? Why am I just hearing about this now?"

This time, the Sister Anne Marie look was more of a glare. Only an idiot wouldn't have known what that meant. I lifted a hand to my lips and mimed a zipping motion. I might have also bounced in my seat once or twice. This story was proceeding at a snail's pace and the suspense was killing me.

"The Gallagher House is located in an older,

three-story home just south of I-95. Indeed, we can hear the rumble of traffic from our living room," Rose told me. "As for *when*, Peter and I returned from Honduras when this property was offered to us with the condition that it be used as a shelter or safe house for women in need of a change of circumstance."

"Battered women," I said.

"Yes, although the more correct terminology now would be victims of domestic violence. Peter and I are simply calling the shelter a place of solace. A home where women in difficult situations can come and find peace."

"And security," I added.

"Amen to that," Aunt Rose agreed.

"This all seems very sudden."

"That's because it was. Our benefactor is a formidable woman named Beatrice Gallagher. You'll meet her. You'll like her, I'm sure. She's a woman who knows what she wants and doesn't waste time getting it."

I nodded. I was acquainted with several women like that. One of them was sitting right in front of me.

"The house she donated for our use was the home where she and her husband, Howard, had lived when they were first married. He went on to make a fortune in the construction business and they moved to a better neighborhood, where they settled down to raise their family. Howard retained this house as an investment property, and until recently it had been on a long-term lease. He passed away a few years ago, so Bea makes the financial decisions now. Once the house became available, she contacted us. Things moved along quite quickly after that."

"She sounds like a very generous woman," I said. "What made her decide to offer the property to you and Peter?"

There was a movement beside my foot. Bud had popped his head out from underneath the couch. He considered that space to be his own private den. Now the little chowhound was probably checking to make sure that I wasn't serving any food.

Rose spared the dog a glance, then lifted her gaze back to me. "Beatrice has always been a firm believer in doing good works. She volunteered at the Stamford Community Center back when Peter was running the Outreach Program there."

"Then they've known each other a long time."

"Quite so. Beatrice relied upon Peter for grief counseling after Howard died. She trusts him implicitly. He even keeps a spare key to her house for her. The offer grew from the strength of that relationship."

"Good for him," I said. "How long has the shelter been open?"

"Barely a month, but already we have several women in residence. So even in a well-to-do community like this one, the need was obviously there. Our population won't be static, however. Some women will need transitional housing, a place to live while they put their lives back together. Others will stay for a few days while they explore their options." Rose paused to frown. "Then there are those who show up in a panic one night and are gone by the next morning."

"Back to the situation they were running from?"

She nodded unhappily.

"Do you and Peter provide counseling services?"

"We certainly do." Rose brightened. "That's Peter's bailiwick, of course. In addition, we offer access to legal aid and continuing education courses. Our doors are open to anyone who needs us. Women with young children are welcome too."

Realization dawned. "Those are the children you were talking about."

"Indeed."

I shook my head. "I can't believe you and Peter have been working on all this, right here in Stamford, and I had no idea. How could I not have known about it?"

"In the first place," Rose replied tartly, "this city has more than a hundred thousand residents. And your home here in North Stamford and the Gallagher House on the south side of the city are literal miles apart. That's plenty of space for both of us to go about our business without tripping over one another. And in the second place"—her gaze sharpened—"you never inquired about what Peter and I were up to."

The comment was intended to make me feel guilty. And it succeeded.

"That's because I thought the two of you were still in Central America," I said in my own defense. *Or Africa,* I added silently.

"We had cell service in Honduras," Rose pointed out. "Not that I remember receiving any calls from you."

"I thought you were busy," I mumbled.

"We were," Rose snapped. "Peter and I were busy helping people who have access to few of the many advantages that you so blithely take for granted. And now I would like you to do one small thing to help children in need for whom a visit from the Easter Bunny would seem like it was nothing less than magical. Is that too much to ask?"

When she put it that way, of course not.

"What do you want me to do?" I asked.

Faith glanced up at me and wagged her tail, signaling her approval. I reached over and settled a hand on top of her withers, massaging her favorite spot at the base of her neck.

"At the moment, we have three young children staying with us," Rose replied. "All of them are old enough to have celebrated the Easter holiday in the past and to know that it's coming up shortly. Yesterday I overheard one boy tell his mother that he didn't want to stay at the shelter because the Easter Bunny wouldn't be able to find him there."

A lump welled up in my throat. I bit back a sniffle, then sighed.

"Whatever you need," I said. "Count me in."

"Excellent. How are you at hard boiling eggs?"

"Thoroughly competent. They're one of the things I cook best."

"Davey and Kevin can help you with the coloring of the eggs," Rose decided. "They'll enjoy that. I want everything to look bright and festive. The Easter egg hunt needs to be a big treat for the children, since it has to make up for the holiday celebrations they'll be missing at home. Three dozen eggs should do it, don't you think?"

"That'll be more than enough," I told her. "But if you're going to play Easter Bunny, you can't just give the kids hard boiled eggs. They'll also need baskets filled with chocolates, jelly beans, and marshmallow Peeps."

"I quite agree. You can be in charge of that part, too."

I supposed I'd walked right into that.

"I'll be offering an additional prize to the child who finds the most eggs," Rose said, standing up. "A live bunny with floppy ears. Afterward, the rabbit will live at the shelter so all the children can enjoy it. But the winner will get to hold the bunny first and choose its name."

"That sounds perfect," I said.

Faith's tail was wagging again. She liked that idea too.

The other dogs had fallen asleep around us while we'd been chatting. When I rose to my feet, Eve opened her eyes and extended her front legs in a long, leisurely stretch. Tar was on the floor next to my feet. He lifted his head as I stepped carefully over him. Then he rolled over and went back to sleep.

Rose and I walked to the front door together. "I'll text you the address for the Gallagher House," she told me. "What are you doing to-morrow?"

I shrugged. It was spring break. The only thing on my schedule was sleeping late. After that, my day was free.

"Come by in the morning and I'll show you around," Rose said. "Once you've seen the lay-out, you can start making plans for the Easter egg hunt. Beatrice will be stopping by too. She said there was something she wanted to discuss with Peter and me. I'd love for the two of you to get to know one another. She's an interesting woman."

"I can't wait to meet her," I said.

Rose pulled on her jacket and let herself out.

I watched through the front window as she backed her minivan carefully down the driveway and onto the road. Faith had followed me out to the front hall. She stood up on her hind legs and braced her front paws on the sill so she could see too.

"I'm not boring," I told her.

Faith woofed under her breath. She didn't sound convinced.

"I'm not," I said again.

The Poodle dropped to all fours in front of the door. She lifted her muzzle to nudge the doorknob with her nose. That message was clear.

Show me!

I glanced back in the direction of the living room. The other Poodles were all up now. Bud came scooting out from under the couch. The canine crew was heading our way. I was about to be outnumbered. And probably outvoted too. Apparently I was taking the dogs for a walk.

I grabbed a leash off the side table and snapped it onto Bud's collar. As I got a coat out of the closet, the little dog gave me a baleful look. I shot one right back.

"The Poodles listen to me," I said. "You don't."

Bud wagged his tail anyway. He was cute and he knew it.

"Do you promise to pay attention when I call you?"

A noise sounded behind me. It sounded suspiciously like a snort. Faith was probably laughing. She knew as well as I did that Bud's promises were mostly meaningless.

The Poodle pack was swarming around my

legs. They were ready to go. I was the only one holding us back.

"You'll keep Bud out of trouble, right?" I asked.

Five pomponned tails lifted in the air. They waved back and forth in unison. As if we were all in agreement that the Poodles would make that happen.

I sighed, then grasped the doorknob and turned it. It was one thing to be outmaneuvered by Aunt Rose. But even worse when it was my dogs who had the upper hand.

Chapter
Three

Stamford, Connecticut, is a bustling suburban city. Outside the downtown area, however, are numerous small, cozy neighborhoods. In North Stamford, where I lived with my family, houses were set back from the road on tree-lined lots. Sidewalks were mostly empty, and kids could skateboard in the street without having to worry about dodging traffic. We loved it there.

Even though our dogs could run around in our fenced backyard anytime they wanted, they still enjoyed going on long walks. Tar was our older male Poodle. Predictably, he was the first one out the door. Tall and handsome, he'd had a successful career in the show ring with Sam.

Right on Tar's heels was our other male Poodle, Augie. He was Davey's dog, and he hated to be bested by Tar in anything. Those two ruffians were joined by Bud. The trio raced each other to the curb, where they slid to a stop and sniffed their way around a maple tree.

Faith, Eve, Plum, and I followed the boys at a more civilized pace. The two older bitches had taken it upon themselves to educate Plum in the ways of the world. She was still a puppy, however, so I still needed to keep an eye on her. Despite Eve's and Faith's efforts, Plum wasn't a solid citizen yet.

All of our adult Standard Poodles were retired show champions. They wore their coats clipped short, with a thick blanket of curls covering their bodies and legs, a rounded topknot on their heads, and a plush pompon at the end of their tails. That made it easy for me to pick out Plum from a distance. She was apparently the one who looked like a woolly bear.

The lap around our neighborhood was nearly two miles long. The Poodles all ran and played together. They were having a fine time. Even Bud was behaving himself for once. It was a beautiful day to be outside. The sun was shining and the temperature was nearing fifty. We'd had snow just two weeks earlier. Now it felt like spring weather might be right around the corner.

One of our neighbors had decorated a tree in

their yard by hanging dozens of brightly colored Easter eggs from its branches. Another had a trio of large, pastel-colored bunnies peeping out from behind their front bushes. Our nod to the upcoming holiday was the floral Easter wreath, which Kevin had made at school, that now graced our front door.

As the dogs and I approached our house, I saw Sam's SUV coming down the road from the other direction. I gathered the Poodles to my side, then quickly picked up Bud before he could dart away. The little guy squirmed in my arms when Sam waved and tooted the horn. That was enough to send all the Poodles flying toward home.

I waited until Sam was parked before releasing Bud to follow them. The spotted dog's feet were already paddling in the air before he even reached the ground. Then he was gone in a flash.

By the time I reached the back of the driveway, the Poodle welcoming committee had already swarmed the SUV. Sam must have stopped on his way home to pick up Kevin from his playdate. Our younger son's head, with its shaggy blond hair, was barely visible at the bottom of the rear window.

Kev had turned six a few weeks earlier. He'd also recently graduated to using a booster seat in the car, which made him feel very grown-up. But when he threw open the back door, jumped out, and came racing toward me with both arms outstretched, all I could see was the little boy who sometimes still let me hold him on my lap.

"Mom-eee!" he cried.

I started to smile, then abruptly realized Kevin wasn't wearing his coat. When he drew closer, I saw that his arms and hands were liberally covered with what looked like blue paint. There was a bright smear of yellow across his shirt, and his bangs were tipped with red. I was used to cleaning up unexpected messes. Even so, my paint-splattered son was an arresting sight.

Quickly I stuck out a hand with which to hold him at bay. Thankfully, Kev's exuberant dash halted before he could wrap his arms around my waist.

"Whoa," I said. "What happened to you?"

"Lydia Martin says it's finger paint." Poodles eddying around his legs, Sam stepped around from the other side of the SUV. Fine lines crinkled on either side of his sky blue eyes as he tried unsuccessfully to smother a grin. We'd been married eight years and the man still gave me palpitations. "She also said that it washes off."

I stared at Kevin dubiously. "And you believed her?"

"It's not like I had a choice," Sam pointed out. "I had to bring the kid home."

"Yeah, we did." Davey laughed as he hopped

out of the SUV. Fifteen years old, he was currently navigating the no-man's-land between childhood and adulthood. His voice had just dropped several octaves and he was angling for Sam and me to let him get a tattoo. That was definitely not happening on my watch. "If you want, I can squirt him with the hose."

"Yay!" Kevin's head whipped around, and he held up his hands. "Do it! Do it!"

"No way," I said sternly, even though I was pretty sure Davey was joking. "No water. No hoses. It's still winter out here. The outside faucets aren't even turned on yet."

"I can fix that," Davey said.

"I can fix you," I told him.

He sidled over to stand beside me. Davey had shot past me in height and he was still growing. Now he had to gaze downward to look me in the eye. "You think?"

"I do," I retorted. "In fact I know I can."

"Big words from a small woman," Davey replied. "You want to arm wrestle?"

I shook my head. The kid was incorrigible. But since he took after me, I couldn't really complain.

"No, I don't want to arm wrestle."

Davey grinned. He thought he'd won.

"But here's a thought. Rather than thinking of me as a short person, try thinking of me as the person who controls your phone access."

Davey doesn't have a poker face. I watched

him process the comment, and knew the moment it hit home.

"Oh." He took a hasty step back. "Yes, ma'am. Anything you say."

From behind my son's back, Sam gave me a thumbs up. I resisted the temptation to take a small bow. Davey might be taller than I was, but he hadn't succeeded in outsmarting me yet.

"You're dumb." Kevin pointed at his brother. "Her name isn't *ma'am*. It's *Mom*."

I started to correct him. In our family, we didn't call each other dumb.

Then I had a better idea. I strode over to where Sam was standing and gave him a quick hug. When I stepped back, I smiled. "Your turn."

From the outside, the Gallagher House didn't look at all like I'd expected. The building appeared no different than the other residences on the short street. It was tall and narrow, and wedged onto a tiny plot of land that consisted mostly of dirt and driveway. The structure's clapboard siding was worn in spots and its second- and third-story windows needed a good cleaning. A narrow, covered porch ran the length of the residence.

"It just looks like a house," I said. Aunt Rose and I were standing on the sidewalk out front the next morning. Considering its current use, I'd pictured a more commercial building.

"It *is* a house, dear," Rose replied. "I told you that yesterday, didn't I?"

"I guess so."

"From the outside no one would suspect what we're doing here. A casual passerby wouldn't look twice at us. And being able to blend into our surroundings is a good thing."

I hadn't considered that aspect. "Does that make it easier for you to stay safe?"

Rose shrugged. "There's always the possibility one might have to deal with an irate boyfriend or husband."

I glanced up and down the street. "How do your neighbors feel about that?"

"Peter made a point of talking to everyone who lives nearby before we moved in. You know how good he is at connecting with people and smoothing things along."

I nodded. During his earlier tenure as a priest, Peter had earned advanced degrees in both counseling and social work. He was not only a wonderful listener, he was equally adept at dispensing advice. I could easily imagine him putting the neighbors at ease.

"Peter informed everyone of our mission, told them about the good work we hoped to accomplish and asked if they had any questions or suggestions. Some people were surprised, of course. But in the end, most were very supportive. I think they appreciate what we're doing. As you can see, this isn't the best neighborhood."

No, it wasn't. The houses around us appeared to date from the middle of the previous century. Many were in a state of disrepair. One had a warped wooden plank propping up the roof of its porch. The sidewalk that ran the length of the street was cracked and buckled. And even though windows were closed to ward off the chilly March air, I could still hear the thumping beat of the loud music that was playing in the house next door. Surrounded by other, similar neighborhoods that had been gentrified, this one had apparently been skipped over, perhaps because of its proximity to the busy highway.

Two motorcycles, mufflers removed, came roaring down the street behind us. I dodged the spray of gravel that was kicked up by their wheels. Aunt Rose watched complacently as the two bikes braked, then went skidding into a small paved area in front of a house several doors down. Two teenage boys, neither wearing a helmet, hopped off the bikes and went inside.

"Even though it's inevitable that we have people coming and going here—sometimes at odd hours—we are by contrast quiet neighbors," she told me. "We do our best to cause no disruptions. We mind our own business. And fortunately, those around us seem inclined to do the same."

"Let's go inside," I said. "I'd love for you to show me around."

As we approached the front steps, the door

opened and Peter came striding out. I hadn't seen him in several years—not since before he and Rose had left for their sojourn in Central America. Peter hadn't changed much in the interim. He looked like he'd lost some weight, but this more slender look suited him.

Peter was a few years older than Rose, probably nearing seventy. His ginger brown hair was thinning on top and shot through with gray. The tortoiseshell glasses perched on his nose were new, but his face still had that wonderful, comfortable quality that made people warm to him immediately.

He'd come skipping down the steps before he noticed me and Rose standing there. Then Peter's face broke out in a big smile. "Melanie, is that really you?"

"It is indeed." I was smiling too. "Hello, Peter."

He threw his arms open wide and gathered me into a bear hug that was long enough to banish the March chill. Finally, his hands still resting on my shoulders, Peter stepped back and held me at arm's length.

"You're looking good," he said. "Really good. Everything's well with you and your family?"

"Couldn't be better," I told him.

"Excellent. Glad to hear that. I'm sorry to run off, but I have an appointment. If I'd known you were coming . . ." He glanced at Rose.

"That's all right," I said quickly. "I didn't know myself until yesterday. We'll catch up another time, okay?"

"Count on it," Peter replied. The silver minivan Rose had been driving the day before was parked at the curb. He hopped behind the wheel and took off.

"He looks well," I said to Rose.

"Mmhmm." She stared after her husband thoughtfully.

I turned back to the house. From the foot of the steps, I could see a discreet plaque affixed to the wall beside the front door: GALLAGHER HOUSE. Then I realized that Rose wasn't beside me and glanced back.

"Is everything okay?"

"Yes, of course." She strode past me to lead the way. "Peter always has a dozen different things going on at once. I just wish that sometimes I could get him to slow down. Let's go inside, shall we?"

Chapter
Four

Someone had lavished the interior of the Gallagher House with all the care and attention that appeared to be missing on the outside. Hardwood floors were buffed. Framed pictures hung on the walls. And a bowl of fresh flowers filled the air with fragrance.

A narrow center hallway was flanked by a steep staircase that led up to the second floor. One side of the hall opened out into a living room, where multiple couches and chairs took up much of the available space. There was a flat screen TV above the mantelpiece and four windows let in plenty of light. The back wall held a tall bookcase that was overflowing with books, magazines, and children's games.

Two women were seated at a small table with a laptop open between them. They glanced up with mild interest when we paused in the doorway, then returned to what they were doing when Rose pulled me away.

"The dining room is over here." She ushered me across the hall. A long wooden table filled the center of the room. It was surrounded by eight mismatched chairs. "We offer three meals a day, served family style."

"Who cooks?" I asked curiously.

"Most days, I do. And Peter sometimes pitches in. Some of the women enjoy cooking for us too, so that makes a pleasant change. At the moment, we're running on a bit of a shoe-string, but we've applied for grant money and government assistance. Once that comes through, the plan will be to hire a full time cook and housekeeper."

No wonder Rose had asked for my help. Running this place, even now when it was still nearly empty, had to be a full-time job. And neither she nor Peter was as young as they used to be.

"The kitchen is behind the dining room," she continued. "There's a small basement apartment so Peter and I have our own separate living quarters, but we've converted the storage room, that's next to the kitchen, into our office."

"What about upstairs?" I walked toward the staircase and peered upward. I was beginning to realize that the Gallagher House was a good deal bigger than I'd first thought. "How many rooms are up there?"

"There are three bedrooms and a bathroom on the second floor, with an additional bedroom and half bath on the third. We've not been pressed for space yet, but if things get tight, we can put the attic to use if we have to."

"Where do you want the egg hunt to take place?" It certainly looked like I wouldn't have a problem finding enough places to hide all the colored eggs. "Will it be just downstairs or upstairs too? And what about outside?"

"Let's step into my office and discuss it." Rose led the way to the end of the hallway. She opened the door to a small room and switched on a light.

Considering the office's former use, it wasn't surprising that the space inside was cramped. A desk that would have looked at home in a schoolroom was pushed against the back wall. A computer sat open on top of it. There was a tall rubber plant in one corner and a pile of cardboard boxes in another. The only seating in the room was provided by two plain wooden chairs. Rose and I each chose one and sat down.

We spent the next half hour making plans. Weather permitting, eggs would be concealed both inside the house and outside in the small yard. Hiding places indoors would be limited to the public rooms on the ground floor—but other than that, any spot I could come up with was fair game.

"As long as you make sure all the eggs are thoroughly hard-boiled," Rose said. "I don't want to find myself cleaning runny yolks off the walls or the furniture."

"Absolutely," I agreed.

"I assume you will want to spend the holiday with your family, so you may leave all the supplies with me the night before, along with those other things you mentioned. Jelly beans and chocolate rabbits, I believe?"

"Just leave all that to me," I told her. "I'll drop off everything you need at the same time." I already planned to shop for holiday supplies for two children. It wouldn't be any trouble at all to triple my order.

I was reaching for the jacket that I'd hung over the back of my chair when Rose glanced down at her watch and frowned. "That's odd."

"What is?"

"I was expecting Beatrice to meet us here this morning. She wanted to talk to me about something, and I was eager to tell her about our Easter plans."

"Maybe she got held up," I said.

Rose's cell phone was on the desk. She leaned over and picked it up. "Beatrice is usually very reliable. It's not like her to miss an appointment. I'll just give her a call."

As Rose held the phone to her ear, there was

a tentative knock on the office door. I stood up and went to open it. One of the women whom I'd seen in the living room was standing there. She looked uncomfortable interrupting us. She was chewing on her lower lip and her hands were twined tightly together in front of her.

The woman didn't say a word to me. Instead she peered over my shoulder, looking for Rose. "Mrs. Donovan? There's someone here to see you."

"Oh, good." Rose set down the phone and got up. "That must be Beatrice now. Thank you, Rachel. I'll be right out."

"Umm, no." She grimaced as though reluctant to convey the rest of the message. "It's a man that's here. He says he's from the police."

I stifled a gasp, then spun around to look at Rose. She appeared to be as shocked as I was.

When she spoke, her voice wasn't quite steady. "Are you sure?"

"That's what he said. He isn't wearing a uniform, but he showed me a badge."

"I'll come right away." Two quick steps brought Rose to my side. Her fingers closed over my arm. Her grasp was tight enough to hurt.

"Not Peter," she whispered. The words sounded like a prayer.

"I'm sure Peter is fine," I said with more confidence than I felt. "We just saw him. This is about something else."

Rachel stepped back out of the way, leaving

our path clear. The front door to the house was closed, and no one was waiting for us in the hallway. She must have shown the policeman into the living room.

Rose still didn't move. It was as if she were frozen in place.

"Do you want me to go talk to him?" I asked.

"No." She shook her head. "No. I'm all right. I'll see to it. You'll come with me."

It was an order, not a request, but I was happy to comply. Even if I hadn't been curious, there was no way I could leave Rose on her own. Whatever the officer had to say, she and I would face it together.

Rose and I were side by side when we rounded the corner into the living room. The other woman who'd been there earlier had disappeared. I didn't blame her. In my experience, an unexpected visit from the police never boded well.

A heavyset man was standing near the fireplace, waiting for us. His feet were braced wide apart, his hands hung at his sides. He'd unbuttoned his topcoat, but hadn't taken it off. His stern face, with its bushy brows and square jaw, assumed a deliberately neutral expression.

I recognized him right away: Detective Sturgill, of the Stamford Police Department. In the past, he and I had occasionally found ourselves working together—or at least comparing notes. Our collaborations hadn't always been mutually agreeable, but I liked to think that we'd developed a grudging respect for each other's opinions.

Sturgill's brow rose at the sight of me. "Ms. Travis? I hadn't expected to find you here."

I crossed the room and offered him my hand. The detective seemed slightly taken aback by that. It took him a moment to respond. When he did, I could feel the calluses on his palm as we shook.

"Rose Donovan is my aunt," I said. "Anything you have to say to her, you can tell me."

Sturgill glanced at Rose. She nodded.

"Perhaps we should take a seat," he said.

Rose was too impatient for that. "Is something wrong?" she asked. "Is it Peter?"

"Peter?" The detective frowned.

"Peter Donovan, my husband." On suddenly boneless legs, she sank into a nearby armchair. "Did something happen to him? Is that why you're here?"

"No." Sturgill was still frowning. "I don't know anything about Mr. Donovan. This is with regard to another matter."

"Oh, thank God," Rose exhaled heavily.

I perched on the arm of the chair and rubbed my aunt's back as she pulled herself together. Her reaction to the detective's appearance seemed surprisingly emotional for the stern, resolute woman I knew her to be.

Detective Sturgill sat down opposite us on the

couch. "Maybe Ms. Travis could get you a drink of water?"

"No, I'm fine." Rose managed a weak smile. Now that she knew her husband was safe, she quickly regained her composure. "Please continue."

This time the detective's gaze came my way to seek approval. I nodded. I wanted to hear what he had to say too.

"I believe you are acquainted with a woman named Beatrice Gallagher?"

"Yes, of course." Rose's head came up. She hadn't expected that. "Beatrice is a dear friend. In fact, she's the person who donated the use of this house, enabling us to open the women's shelter."

"This is a shelter?" Sturgill sounded surprised. He gazed around the room, then looked back at us.

"We haven't been open long," Rose told him. "The Stamford Police Department is well aware that we're here. My husband, Peter, made sure to notify the local authorities, as well as all the churches and religious agencies in the area. We've already received a referral or two from your law enforcement agency."

"Is that so?" Sturgill hated to be caught out. I wouldn't want to be the person who'd neglected to mention that tidbit of information before sending him our way. "I'll make a note of that."

"You mentioned Beatrice a moment ago," Rose said. "Is she all right?"

Sturgill took a deep breath before answering. "No, ma'am, I'm sorry to have to tell you that she isn't. Mrs. Gallagher passed away early this morning from a fall inside her home."

"A fall?" Rose stared at him in disbelief. "How could such a thing happen? Beatrice is every bit as sturdy as you or I. Why would she fall?"

"I'm afraid I don't know the answer to that."

"Was she ill?"

"Again," Sturgill replied, "I don't yet have that information."

I looked at the detective across the room. He was seated on the edge of the couch, his sharp gaze focused on Aunt Rose as he watched her process the news. Maybe he was telling us the truth, and he didn't possess much information yet. But I was pretty sure Sturgill suspected something. Otherwise, why would he be here?

"I believe you had a meeting scheduled with Mrs. Gallagher this morning," he said to Rose.

"Yes, I did."

"Could you tell me what it was about?"

"I don't know. She simply said there was something she wanted to discuss. I was delighted she'd be coming by. I wanted to show her the improvements we'd made since her last visit. And I wanted to introduce her to Melanie."

His eyes shifted my way, even as he continued

to question Rose. "Why would you want to do that?"

"They're both stimulating women. I thought they would enjoy getting to know one another." Rose paused, then added, "Plus, there's the Easter egg hunt."

"That's where I come in," I said. I knew Sturgill would ask. I might as well save him the effort.

"You." He sounded bemused. "Doing *what?*"

I lowered my voice before replying. Presumably, none of the children were nearby. But if they heard me confess to playing Easter Bunny on their behalf, it would ruin the surprise.

"I'm coordinating Easter baskets and an Easter egg hunt for the kids who are currently in residence here," I told him. Sturgill still looked perplexed. "You know, because Easter's coming?"

"I'm aware that Easter's coming, Ms. Travis."

"Good," I said. "Then we're both on the same page."

"And neither of you has any idea what Mrs. Gallagher wanted to see Mrs. Donovan about this morning?"

"I'm afraid not," I answered. Rose shook her head.

"Then I guess I'll be going." Detective Sturgill braced his hands on his knees and pushed himself to his feet. "Mrs. Donovan, I'm sorry for the loss of your friend."

"Thank you," she replied without looking up.

"I'll show the detective out," I told her.

He and I walked to the door together. When Sturgill stepped out onto the porch, I followed him. He paused to button his coat. And also because I was deliberately standing in his way.

"There's something you weren't saying in there," I said. "How did Mrs. Gallagher actually die?"

"Like I said, she had a fall."

"But you don't think it was an accident."

A half smile tweaked the corners of his mouth. "Ms. Travis, you have a suspicious mind."

"So do you," I replied. "And I'm guessing something's bugging you about how the fall happened. Or else you wouldn't be asking questions."

"Could be you're right." He stepped around me and started down the stairs. "Let's just say I'll neither confirm nor deny that I have doubts until I have more information."

He hadn't answered my question—but his evasion was an answer in itself.

"Fair enough," I said.

Chapter
Five

When I went back inside, Rose was still sitting where I'd left her. She was staring toward a window in the back wall of the room, but her gaze had a hazy, unfocused quality. Her thoughts appeared to be turned inward.

"Are you all right?" I asked.

She glanced up, and looked almost surprised to see me.

"No. How can I be all right after hearing news like that? Poor Beatrice. What a horrible thing to have happen. She was a fine woman. She didn't deserve to have her life cut short."

Rose's breath caught on a sob. "Her children must be devastated. First they lost their father, and now this."

"Tell me about Beatrice's family," I said. Maybe it would help her to talk.

"I'd be happy to. But why don't we relocate to Peter's and my apartment? I have a feeling everyone is hiding upstairs because they don't wish to disturb us. Let's get out of their way."

"Good idea," I agreed. That would give us more privacy too.

Under the stairway in the hall was a small door I hadn't previously noticed. As Rose and I walked toward it, three women leaned out over the second-floor banister above us. One was Rachel. Like the two women beside her, she looked worried.

"Is everything all right, Mrs. Donovan?" she asked.

"Yes," Rose replied. "There's nothing for you to be concerned about."

I wouldn't characterize things that way myself, I thought. But maybe Rose didn't want to alarm the residents until she knew what was going to happen next.

"Detective Sturgill has left," she added. "Melanie and I will be downstairs if anyone needs me."

The enclosed staircase that led to the lower floor was carpeted and well lit. At the bottom, Rose and I were confronted by another door.

"When Beatrice and Howard lived in this house, this was a finished basement," she explained. "After they moved on, Howard converted the space into a separate apartment to maximize his rental income. As you can imagine, it's useful for Peter and me to be on hand, yet still have our own living quarters."

Rose opened the door and led the way into a spacious room that served as both a living and dining area. Kitchen appliances were lined up along one wall and a row of high windows just below the ceiling let in a good amount of light. Another door, on the far side of the room, led to the outside.

"There's also a small bedroom and bath," Rose told me as she headed toward the kitchen. "It probably doesn't look like much to you, but compared to the leaky hut Peter and I lived in for six months in Honduras, this feels positively palatial to us. Would you like a cup of coffee?"

"I'd love one." I walked over to admire a ceramic bowl that appeared to be pre-Colombian. "This is lovely."

Rose glanced back over her shoulder. "Don't let Peter hear you say that. He'll talk your ear off if you show even the slightest bit of interest. He fancies himself a collector. Not the really expensive stuff, of course. But he does manage to acquire a quality piece every now and then."

Rose shut the refrigerator door and walked toward me with a steaming mug in each hand. She held one out to me. "Just a dash of milk, right?"

"Right. You have a good memory."

I couldn't remember the last time she and I had shared a cup of coffee. Actually, I couldn't remember the last time Aunt Rose and I had shared much of anything. That was beginning to seem like a shame.

Two overstuffed chairs sat across from each other, with a low table in between them. Rose set out a pair of coasters and we each took a seat.

"You were going to tell me about Beatrice's family," I said.

"Yes, although there isn't much to tell. Peter and I first crossed paths with Beatrice and Howard quite a while ago at a charitable event. Once we started talking to Bea, it quickly became clear that we were on the same page about wanting to help people who were less fortunate. Howard didn't necessarily agree. He was a gruff, tough man. With what he did for a living, he probably had to be. I think I told you he made his money in construction?"

I nodded.

"But he clearly loved Beatrice and she adored him in return. Howard would joke about how hard he had to work to make his money, and how fast she was able to spend it for him. He could never resist indulging her."

I took a sip of my coffee. It was rich and strong. "You said that they had children?"

"Yes, two. A son and a daughter, Charlie and Cherise. They're both in their late twenties now.

Howard died"—she stopped and thought back—
"almost three years ago. Cancer. He fought it for
more than a year, so there was time for him to
think about and decide upon the financial arrangements he wanted to make. Apparently, there
was a blazing row between him and Charlie
when Howard was ill. Charlie wanted to take over
the construction business, and his father thought
he was too young and inexperienced. He ended
up selling it instead."

Families. I sighed. In my experience, almost
everything about being part of one was difficult.

"I hope that didn't end up tearing them
apart," I said.

"It might have done," Rose conceded. "But
then Howard died shortly thereafter, and all was
forgiven as the remaining family members came
together in their shared grief."

"Now they've lost their mother as well," I said
with a frown. "They're young to have to deal
with the loss of both parents."

"Yes, they are," Rose agreed. "Charlie and
Cherise share an apartment in a high-rise downtown. I think I'll call and check on them to
make sure there's nothing they need. Peter and
I owe it to their mother to take an interest in
their well-being."

"You were planning to see Beatrice this morning," I mentioned.

"Yes."

"You told Detective Sturgill you didn't know

what she wanted to talk to you about. Was that the truth?"

"Of course. Bea didn't give me so much as a clue over the phone. At the time, I thought it didn't matter because she and I would be seeing each other soon."

I paused for another sip, then said, "I was wondering if you really didn't know what Beatrice wanted or if you just didn't want to tell the detective."

Rose looked seriously affronted. "I would never lie to a policeman."

Once again, I was reminded that my aunt was a former nun. After three decades in the convent, she had to be well versed in the commandments and the weight they were meant to carry in everyday life. She probably wouldn't lie to anyone. Hopefully that included me.

"One last thing," I said. "You told me Beatrice donated this house for you and Peter to turn into a women's shelter."

"That's correct."

"Did she retain ownership, or did she sign the deed over to you and Peter?"

"No, the house doesn't belong to us," Rose replied. "This property was the first thing Bea and Howard purchased together many years ago. She still has . . . she *had* . . . a sentimental attachment to it. That was one reason she wanted to be sure that it was put to good use."

"So you and Peter must have signed a lease."

"Well, no." She frowned. "There was no need. We were all in full agreement about how everything was going to proceed. The three of us were working together, almost as partners. There was no reason to bog things down with paperwork."

Maybe not at the time, I thought. *But now, suddenly, everything has changed.*

I gave her a moment to think about that as I finished the last of my coffee. "Do you think that will be a problem?"

"No," she replied firmly. "The house will most likely go to Charlie and Cherise. I'm sure they'll understand the importance of the work we're doing here."

I wasn't nearly as convinced of that as Rose was. I hoped for her sake I was wrong.

My plan for Sunday was to spend a quiet day at home with my husband and kids.

Sam and Davey gathered all the supplies they needed to work on the tree house and headed outside. Kevin, who'd appointed himself chief hammer-holder, trailed along behind. Bud and the Poodles were already out in the backyard too. I grabbed an outdoor chair from the garage, where they'd been stored for the winter, then went out to supervise from the deck.

The temperature was cool, but there wasn't a single cloud in the sky. The sun, shining brightly overhead, quickly warmed the air. After only a few minutes, I'd already taken off my jacket.

Faith was sitting beside me on the deck. Her beautiful head was resting in my lap, and my fingers were rubbing her ears. Now ten years old, Faith's days of boisterous play with the Poodle pack were behind her. Her muzzle was more gray than black, and her first few steps each morning were stiff with age.

None of that seemed to matter, however, when she and I could still share a common thought, a laughing glance, or even a conversation. The big Poodle and I had been best friends for a decade. I hoped we still had many more years together ahead of us.

At the other end of the yard, the other dogs were engaged in a spirited game of tag. Tar and Augie were the two ringleaders. Bud, with his much shorter legs, had to cut across the Poodles' big, looping circles in order to keep up. I kept a careful eye trained on Plum. As the only Poodle currently "in hair" it was imperative that she not engage in any games that would put her growing show coat at risk.

Sam had already carried the ladder and a toolbox over to the huge old oak tree in the center of the yard. Davey was bringing the lumber. Kevin had his hammer and a sealed box of nails. The three of them set up shop on the ground beside the tree's broad trunk.

Above them, the tree house was wedged in a

fork between two spreading branches that were eight feet off the ground. Since the tree was bare of leaves, access was easier now than it would be in a month or two. Even so, I suspected that Sam and Davey would be working for most of the afternoon.

"Let me know if you guys need any help," I called from the comfort of my wicker seat.

"Yeah, right." Davey smirked. "We all know you don't like heights."

"No, but I could stand on the ground and hand you things."

"Hey!" Kevin shot me an outraged look. "That's my job."

"You see?" said a voice behind me. "I knew you didn't have anything to do this week. It's a good thing Rose came up with something to keep you busy."

I whipped around in surprise. Naturally, I'd recognized Aunt Peg's voice. I just hadn't been expecting to hear it this morning.

She was standing outside the gate that led from the driveway to the backyard. Tall and ramrod straight, Aunt Peg was a formidable woman in every sense of the word. She'd bulldozed her way through her first seven decades of life, and she obviously had no intention of slowing down anytime soon.

Of course there was a black Standard Poodle puppy dancing around her legs. Aunt Peg had long been recognized as an expert in the breed.

Over the years, her Cedar Crest Kennel had produced generations of black Standard Poodles that were renowned for the quality of their conformation, temperaments, and health.

Aunt Peg had recently mourned the loss of her oldest Poodle, Beau. He'd been king of her kennel for many years. Now busy with a judging career that took her all over the world, she no longer bred many litters. When she did have puppies, however, the results were always something special.

Aunt Peg's most recent litter had been born the previous summer. Sam and I had whelped the puppies for her. When the litter was three months old, Sam and Peg had each chosen a puppy to keep for themselves.

Now I immediately recognized Plum's litter brother, Joker. Nose pressed between the slats of the gate, the black Poodle was a little powerhouse. He was every bit as endearing and as lively as his sister. It was clear he couldn't wait to come in and join the fun.

We hadn't been expecting Aunt Peg, but she'd never been one to wait for an invitation. Instead she simply did as she pleased, making up her own rules as she went along. Faith had already jumped to her feet and gone to greet the new arrivals. There was nothing for me to do but stand up and follow.

"Why are you waiting out there?" I asked Aunt Peg. "Open the gate and come on in."

Chapter
Six

"That looks like quite a project," Aunt Peg said.

She marched right past me, heading for the middle of the yard, where the men in my family were hard at work. Joker scooted through my legs and went to touch noses with Faith. It was left to me to close and latch the gate behind them.

The rest of the Poodle pack, including honorary member Bud, were already racing toward us from the back of the yard. Having noticed Joker's arrival, they couldn't get here fast enough to check him out.

"No hair pulling," Aunt Peg said sternly. "He'll need that coat next month." She watched the milling dogs just long enough to make sure everyone was obeying her command before striding over to the tree.

"Next month?" I hurried to catch up.

"Saw Mill River Kennel Club," she said. "Laney Garret is judging. Plum and Joker are both going. Sam and I have already discussed it. Do try to keep up, Melanie."

If only, I thought.

Abruptly Aunt Peg stopped walking. She shaded her eyes from the sun as she stared upward into the tree. "Ahoy up there!"

Sam was standing near the top of his ladder. Davey was lying on the floor of the tree house and leaning out the open doorway. The two of them were working on positioning a four-foot wooden plank that would then be nailed into place.

"Ahoy? That's what you say to boats, not trees." Kevin appeared from behind the wide trunk. He doubled over in a fit of giggles. "You're silly, Aunt Peg."

"Be careful he doesn't drop that hammer on your foot," I warned her.

She spared me a momentary glance. "He wouldn't dare."

I rescued the small hammer from Kevin's hand anyway. So far, he hadn't done anything other than carry it around, which was all for the best.

"Good morning, Peg," Sam called down. "Want to come up and help?"

"That depends. What are you doing?"

"Right now, we're reinforcing the support beams," Davey told her. "After that, we might build a new ladder if we have time."

"No, thank you. That doesn't sound like much fun. Melanie and I will sit on the deck and chat while you two"—her eyes dropped to Kevin's level—"you *three* manly types continue with what you're doing."

"Sounds good," Sam said. He and Davey went back to work.

While I went to the garage and brought out another wicker chair, Aunt Peg made herself at home in my kitchen. By the time I got back to the deck, she'd brought a bowl of cold water outside for the canine crew and was handing out peanut butter biscuits all around.

"You'll spoil my dogs," I said, shoving her chair into place.

"Pish," she replied. "I'm related to most of them. They feel like my grandchildren. It's my duty to give them things their parents wouldn't."

Aunt Peg sat down and patted her lap. Bud eyed her suspiciously. Another moment and he'd have taken a flying leap. Thankfully, Joker beat him to it.

At seven months of age, the Poodle puppy was already big. He and Aunt Peg barely fit in the chair together. Nevertheless, they both somehow managed to look pleased with the arrangement.

Once we were settled, Aunt Peg cut straight to the chase. "So," she said, "Rose. Tell me everything."

"You start," I replied. "Among the things you neglected to mention the last time we spoke—like that upcoming dog show—was the fact that Peter and Rose had returned from their stint in Honduras."

"Guatemala," she corrected me.

"Nope. Honduras."

"Really?"

"Really. Didn't you pay attention when she was talking to you?"

"Certainly not," Aunt Peg replied. "I rarely listen to a thing Rose says. The woman drives me batty. You know that."

I did. Years before I was even born, Aunt Peg had married Rose's older brother, Max. Hostilities between the two women had begun shortly thereafter. Rose, already in the convent at the time, had accused Peg of trying to usurp her place in the family. Aunt Peg had responded by calling her new sister-in-law a jealous ninny. She'd contended—correctly to my way of thinking—that Rose had abandoned her place long before Peg even showed up on the scene.

From there, the relationship had gone barreling downhill. The two women had been at loggerheads for as long as I'd known them. No matter that most of their arguments stemmed from a disagreement that was years in the past. When it came to each other's transgressions and shortcomings, Peg and Rose both had memories like elephants.

"And yet she told me that you helped her and Peter find a place to live temporarily when they got back."

"Of course I did." Aunt Peg sniffed. "That was the only way I could ensure they didn't end up anywhere near me."

Sad to say, that made perfect sense to me.

"Rose and Peter have opened a women's shelter in Stamford," I told her.

"So I heard. More good works. Bully for them. That should keep Rose busy—and out of everyone else's hair."

"Not exactly," I commented.

Aunt Peg looked my way. "Oh, right, the Easter egg hunt. I'd quite forgotten all about it."

I sincerely doubted that.

"You volunteered me to help out."

"Better you than me," she said. "Besides, it never occurred to me that you'd say yes."

"What choice did I have after you'd put me on the spot?"

"You always have a choice, Melanie. It's your own fault you can't figure out how to turn anyone down."

"I'll remember that the next time you ask me for something."

"Why on earth would you want to say no to me?" Aunt Peg flicked another glance my way. "My requests are always eminently reasonable. Have I ever asked you to dye a hundred Easter eggs?"

"Thirty-six," I said. "And that's not the point."

"Thirty-six eggs," she replied. "I rest my case."

"It turns out there may be an unexpected complication."

"Is that so?"

Aunt Peg had been watching the Poodles' antics, but now I suddenly had her full attention. There was nothing she enjoyed more than the possibility of complications. Especially when Rose was involved.

"Peter and Rose had a benefactor who helped them get the shelter up and running, a woman named Beatrice Gallagher. That was how they were able to pull everything together so quickly."

"I note your use of the past tense," Aunt Peg said dryly. "Did Rose do something to alienate the poor woman and cause them to lose their funding?"

"No. Beatrice passed away unexpectedly yesterday morning."

Abruptly Aunt Peg swiveled in her seat to face me. The move knocked Joker to one side. Deftly she caught the puppy before he tumbled off her lap. "Don't tell me Rose was responsible for *that.*"

"No, of course not."

"There is no *of course not* about it," Aunt Peg huffed. "Let us not forget that she once accused me of murder."

"Not in those exact words," I pointed out.

"The words she used were not the issue," she snapped. "It was their intent that rankled."

Well, yes. I could see that. But if I let Aunt Peg start airing grievances about Rose, we would be here all day.

"Beatrice died from a fall in her home," I told her.

She considered that. "Was she elderly?"

"I never had a chance to meet her. There was a mention of her passing in the local media. It said she was in her late fifties."

"A spring chicken, then."

Comparatively speaking. It seemed safer not to voice that thought aloud.

"What caused her to fall?" Aunt Peg wanted to know.

"I don't know. I was with Rose at the shelter, and we were waiting for Beatrice to meet us there when Detective Sturgill showed up to deliver the news instead."

"Rodney." She smiled. "Lovely man. He'll do a good job."

"*Rodney?*"

"What do you call him?" she asked mildly.

"Detective Sturgill. And, umm . . . sir."

"That's just silly. Perhaps you should get to know him better."

I doubted that. Frankly, our current level of infrequent interaction seemed just about right to me. Aunt Peg had met the detective two years earlier when he and I had worked together to corner a murderer. But I had no idea she'd kept up their relationship.

"Your friend, *Rodney*, appeared to have some doubts about what might have happened to Beatrice," I said.

"What kind of doubts?"

"He wasn't sure her fall was an accident. But he declined to elaborate beyond that."

"Then you must ask him again," Aunt Peg told me firmly. As if it were just that easy to finagle official information out of a tight-lipped member of the police force.

"Maybe," I said without conviction. "Or maybe I'll just hang around home and enjoy my spring vacation."

Aunt Peg gave Joker a gentle nudge. The puppy hopped down off her lap. Feet braced apart on the deck floor, he gave his thick coat a vigorous shake, then looked up at Peg to see what they were going to do next.

"I'm sure you'll have a wonderful time boiling all those eggs," she said. "I can hardly imagine anything more exciting."

Faith accompanied me as I followed Aunt

Peg and Joker back to the driveway. "I never did get a chance to ask," I said. "Was there a reason you stopped by today?"

"I always have a reason," she told me, pausing beside the gate.

That was a blatant lie if ever I'd heard one. Unless you counted such things as hoping to be invited to dinner, or wanting to stir up trouble, as good reasons.

"On this lovely Sunday morning, I had thought we might give the two puppies a handling lesson in anticipation of the upcoming show. But, of course, I hadn't counted on finding Sam up a tree and you up to your nose in trouble again."

"*Me?*" I grinned. "I'm not in any trouble."

"You've been consorting with your Aunt Rose. Mark my words, nothing good ever comes of that. If you're not in trouble yet, you soon will be."

Aunt Peg opened the gate and sailed through it majestically with Joker in her wake. I closed and latched it behind her. Sometimes it was just easier to let her have the last word.

Aunt Rose called with news that afternoon.

"Bea's children are holding a celebration of life ceremony for their mother," she told me. "I can imagine few people more deserving of such a commemoration than Beatrice Gallagher. It will be Tuesday afternoon at the Parkland Funeral Home."

"I assume you and Peter are going?"

"I'll be attending, but I'm on my own. Unfortunately, Peter has an appointment that can't be rescheduled. I thought you might want to come with me."

I paused for a moment as Aunt Peg's parting words came floating back. "I never had a chance to meet Beatrice. Her family and friends will be strangers to me. I wouldn't want to intrude."

"Nonsense. Beatrice was a lovely, openhearted woman who never met a stranger. I'm sure she'd approve of your putting in an appearance. And Charlie and Cherise will be happy for your support."

"I might be busy on Tuesday afternoon."

"And I might be Mother Teresa," Rose scoffed. "Please, Melanie, won't you do this for me?"

It didn't sound as though I had a choice. "I'd be happy to accompany you," I said. "Is everything all right?"

"Of course," Rose replied quickly, but I wasn't convinced. "Why wouldn't it be?"

"Umm . . . no reason."

"Excellent. Then I'll see you there on Tuesday. Two o'clock sharp."

She ended the connection before I could respond.

Faith had been lying at my feet, listening to our conversation. When I put the phone down, she lifted her head to look at me. Her tail flapped up and down on the floor.

"That was odd," I told her. "I think something's up."

The Poodle tipped her head to one side, working on deciphering my mood. *Something good?*

"I don't know." I frowned. "Possibly not."

Something bad?

"Whatever it is, it's nothing for you to worry about." I leaned down to wrap my arms around her neck.

Faith snuggled into my hug. *I can help!*

"You always help," I told her as I levered myself to my feet. "Let's go outside and see how the guys are coming along with the tree house."

Despite Aunt Peg's warning, there was no point in my worrying about something I didn't even understand yet. I'd find out what Rose needed on Tuesday. And maybe I'd worry about it then.

Chapter
Seven

Parkland Funeral Home was a plain, rectangular building made of dark stucco, and located on a side street in downtown Stamford. Its somber façade suited the business that was conducted within. A sign out front announced that the mortuary had been in business since 1952, and parking was available behind the building.

Aunt Rose arrived before I did. I spotted her silver minivan in the semi-full lot and pulled in beside it. Rose was waiting for me inside her vehicle so she and I could enter the funeral home together. She hopped out before my car had even rolled to a stop.

"You're prompt," she said. "I like that."

Rose was wearing a plain, long-sleeved black

dress with a Peter Pan collar. She'd paired it with low-heeled black pumps. The narrow belt that circled her waist was the outfit's only adornment. Briefly I flashed back to a moment years earlier—the last time I'd seen her dressed in the severe black habit of her order. Then I blinked and the image faded. At least today Rose's hair was visible. Gray and cut short, it hugged her head like a skullcap.

"What?" Rose looked at me curiously.

"Nothing." I quickly closed the car door and locked it.

"You were thinking something."

I'd been educated in Catholic school from kindergarten through twelfth grade. Back then, we students had sometimes suspected that the nuns could read our minds. I wondered if Rose's time in the convent had given her that gift. If so, I might as well come clean.

"Your dress," I said. "It reminded me of your habit."

"Really?" Her gaze drifted downward, as if she was reassessing her choice of outfit. "That certainly wasn't my intent." Unexpectedly, she smiled. "Now that I can wear whatever I want, my wardrobe is filled with color. This is the only black dress I own."

"It looks very nice on you," I said primly.

"False compliments will get you nowhere, my dear. I assure you it's much too late for that."

Rose took off across the parking lot, leaving

me to hurry along behind. Why was it that neither of my tall aunts ever thought about matching their long strides to my much shorter ones?

Inside the building, Rose and I signed our names in a guestbook. After that, we were directed down a quiet corridor to the room where Beatrice Gallagher's service was being held. The space was big enough to host a medium-sized crowd, and twenty or thirty people were already inside. At first glance, I didn't see a single familiar face.

Rose and I stepped through the double doorway together. A long table next to the side wall held refreshments. Chairs were grouped in small seating arrangements for attendees who wanted to sit. For now, everyone was still standing. Those holding conversations were doing so in hushed tones. My first impression was that this didn't look like much of a celebration.

Rose's expression brightened as she spotted someone she knew. "Look, there's Phyllis Woods. She and Beatrice belonged to the same bridge club. You don't mind if I go say hello, do you?"

"Of course not," I told her. *I'll just stand here by the door and look like I don't belong.*

I'd thought I was here to act as moral support for Rose. We hadn't even been here two minutes, however, and already she'd deserted me for someone more interesting. The event suddenly reminded me of every awkward mixer I'd attended in high school. I wondered how long I needed to hang around by myself before slinking out the door wouldn't appear disrespectful to the recently deceased.

I took a few steps into the room and glanced at the display of food. Most of the trays were still untouched. I contemplated picking up a Bible from a nearby table and sitting down to read. The Book of Job was beginning to feel appropriate.

"Good afternoon, Ms. Travis."

I turned at the sound of my name. It was such a relief to see someone I knew that I could have hugged him. Except that the man who'd spoken to me was Detective Sturgill, and that would have been a very poor idea.

Apparently I wasn't the only person lingering at the back of the room.

"I didn't realize you'd be here," I said. "Did you come to pay your respects to Beatrice Gallagher?"

Sturgill merely shrugged.

All right. He was going to make me work for it. I could do that.

"I guess your presence means you've decided that Beatrice's death wasn't an accident?" I hadn't spoken loudly, but the hum of conversation around us was so muted that my comment caused several heads to turn our way.

"You might want to lower your voice," the detective growled under his breath. His meaty fingers closed around my upper arm and he led me to a quiet corner.

"Sorry about that," I said.

He was still glowering. How Aunt Peg had ever managed to get on a first-name basis with this man was beyond me.

"In these situations, we try not to advertise a police presence."

Sure. Like Detective Sturgill was going to blend in.

But he'd given me a second chance, and I wasn't about to blow it. So now, I was whispering. "But I was right, wasn't I?"

"About what?" he asked.

"Seriously? You want me to repeat my question?"

The man's chest rose and fell on a sigh. "No, I guess not. And yes, you were correct."

"So Beatrice wasn't killed in a fall?"

"No, we were right about that part from the beginning. It was the tumble down the stairs that killed her. Fractured skull," Sturgill replied in a low tone. "But the ME found other bruising on Mrs. Gallagher that wasn't consistent with the way she fell and the scene we found in the house when the officers arrived."

"Are you telling me that someone pushed her?"

"Frankly, Ms. Travis, I'm trying very hard not to tell you anything at all. But if you were to draw certain conclusions based on the questions you keep posing, I probably wouldn't waste my time trying to change your mind."

So was that a yes or a no? I couldn't really tell. I decided that meant it had to be a yes.

A yes, with the detective maintaining plausible deniability about the topic of our conversation. Smart man.

"Who did it?" I asked.

"If I knew that, I wouldn't be standing here, talking to you."

Oh. Right.

"All we know at the moment is that someone was unhappy enough about what Mrs. Gallagher was up to to want to put an end to it. Permanently. And as far as we can tell, what she was mostly involved with during the weeks immediately preceding her death was making arrangements for your aunt and her husband to open their women's shelter."

"Surely, you don't think there's a connection?"

That earned me another shrug. "We're still exploring all possibilities. But I'm talking to you today because I want you to give Rose Donovan a message from me. Until we get this wrapped up, you tell her to be careful, okay?"

I gulped, then nodded. For once, I didn't have a single thing to say.

*   *   *

The room had filled up while Detective Sturgill and I were talking. Now everyone quieted as a young man and woman walked over to a microphone sitting atop a low platform. Both had blond hair and slender builds. Both carried themselves with an air of assurance, ignoring the curious eyes that followed them as they crossed the room. I assumed the pair were Beatrice's children.

As the conversations stilled, Rose detached herself from the group she'd been with and returned to my side. "Charlie and Cherise." She confirmed my guess. "They look enough alike to be twins, but Charlie is older by a year. He's very protective of his little sister."

Charlie stepped up to the microphone first. He tapped it with his forefinger and feedback squealed through the speakers positioned around the room.

"Okay." He laughed self-consciously. "I guess that's working. I want to thank you all for coming today to celebrate my mother's life. It means a lot to Cherise and me, and I know Mom would be delighted to see each of you again."

Charlie glanced upward, toward the heavens. "She could be bigger than life, you know?"

Heads nodded. People smiled.

"Knowing her penchant for being in charge, I think she's probably looking down on us right now. No doubt she's saying, 'Charlie, why did you order the salmon for the buffet table? You know salmon doesn't do well when it sits out.' "

A ripple of laughter flowed through the room and Charlie looked gratified by the response. He stepped back and looped an arm around his sister's waist, bringing her forward to take his place. Cherise's fingers grasped the stem of the microphone nervously. She gazed out over the assembled group with a tentative smile.

"I want to add my thanks to my brother's," she said. "Charlie and I hope you've come here not to mourn our mother's passing, but to share your memories of the good times you spent with her. She had a wonderful life and she loved every minute of it. Please feel free to come up and share your thoughts, or to chime in with a story or two."

Charlie leaned in beside her to add, "But no pressure, okay? If you don't feel like speaking, there's always plenty of salmon on the buffet table."

"Those two make a cute team," I said to Rose.

"Mmm," she murmured under her breath.

"What?" I turned to face my aunt.

Several people had already stepped up from the audience. A queue was beginning to form behind the microphone. It looked as though we'd be here for a while.

Rose shook her head. "Now isn't the time."

"You don't like Beatrice's children," I whispered. She hadn't mentioned *that* on Saturday.

Rose looked as though she wished she could slap a piece of tape across my mouth. "I barely know her children," she said sharply. "We'll discuss it later, Melanie."

She turned and strode away, leaving me on my own again. Since I'd never met Beatrice Gallagher, the chances of my going up to say a few words were slim and none. I wandered over to sample the salmon instead. It was actually quite good. With a nod to the upcoming holiday, the dessert tray offered a selection of chocolate bunnies and coconut eggs. I sampled those too.

Charlie's lighthearted introduction had produced the desired effect. Ninety minutes later, people were still crowding around the microphone to reminisce about Beatrice. By then, I was sure I'd put in enough time so I could slip out unnoticed. I went to find Aunt Rose, to tell her I was leaving.

I saw her across the room. She was holding a glass of ginger ale in her hand and talking to a woman I didn't know. As I approached, Charlie and Cherise, who'd been working the room as a pair, came toward the women from the other side. I heard Charlie say something about having a private word with Rose. The second woman nodded and left.

Immediately I quickened my stride to join the small group. Rose saw me coming and gave me a faint smile. It looked as though she might be happy to have some backup.

"Cherise and Charlie," she said, "I'd like you to meet my niece, Melanie Travis. She's going to be helping me with some things at the shelter."

I was? That was news to me. I thought my duties were beginning and ending with the Easter festivities.

We all shook hands and murmured appropriately polite greetings.

"Since you're involved with the shelter, I suppose you might as well hear this too," Charlie said. The words were intended for me, but his gaze remained trained on Rose. "The reading of my mother's will is scheduled for tomorrow morning. At that point, the building the Gallagher House occupies will belong to me. The shelter will be closing. You and the women who are in residence there will need to move out. I will give you two weeks to get everything sorted."

Chapter
Eight

"Two weeks?" I gasped.

Rose's face had gone white. Her hand began to tremble. It looked as though she might drop her drink. I took the glass from her nerveless fingers and set it down on a nearby table.

"And that's me being generous," Charlie said in a low voice. Clearly, he didn't want to be overheard. "I could throw you all out tomorrow afternoon if I wanted."

Cherise winced at her brother's harsh words. She reached over to lay a placating hand on Charlie's arm. Pointedly, he ignored her.

"That's not possible," Rose sputtered.

"I assure you, it is," Charlie replied. "Opening

a women's shelter in a residential area was a bad idea from the beginning. The neighbors there are right to be concerned. If my father was still alive, he never would have allowed such a thing to happen. I'm merely undoing what should never have been done in the first place."

"But the shelter was your mother's idea," Rose said. "She was in favor of everything Peter and I proposed. What you're doing now isn't at all what she would have wanted."

"My mother wasn't a businesswoman," Charlie said. Cherise was chewing on her lip unhappily, but she nodded in reluctant agreement. "Mother was a soft touch for a sob story. And she apparently fell for yours, hook, line, and sinker. That doesn't mean I intend to compound her mistake."

"The Gallagher House isn't a mistake. It's your mother's legacy." Rose straightened her shoulders. Her voice strengthened at the same time. "The shelter fills a void in the social care network. It offers a service the community is badly in need of. Perhaps you're unaware of the good work being done there. If you'd like to come and see what I'm talking about, I'd be happy to show you—"

"That won't be necessary," Charlie said firmly. "I've already made up my mind. My decision is final."

Rose and I shared a look of dismay. Two

weeks to unravel everything she and Peter had so carefully put together was unthinkable. And what about the women who were staying at the shelter now? How would they find another safe place to stay on such short notice?

"Charlie, maybe you and I could discuss this later between ourselves," Cherise said. "After all, it seems to me that I should have a say in what happens too . . ."

Her brother silenced her with a glare. "There's something else," he told Rose.

Good Lord, I thought. *Wasn't that enough?*

"The police have been investigating our mother's accident. It looks like they're searching for someone to blame. Unless you cooperate and leave quietly, I will tell the authorities that Mother had changed her mind about lending her support to the shelter—and that you were aware of that. Mother would have given you the same ultimatum I have, if her untimely death hadn't prevented her from doing so."

"That's not possible." Rose's voice quavered. "Beatrice never had the slightest doubt about her commitment to our cause. Nor did Peter and I."

"I imagine the police will ask you to prove that. It will be your word against ours," Charlie said with a sneer. "Don't make me have to evict you, Mrs. Donovan. I assure you, I can make your life very unpleasant."

My gaze flew to the back of the room where Detective Sturgill had been standing earlier. Of course it was empty now. Where was a cop when you needed one?

Charlie spun on his heel and left. Cherise started to follow him, then turned back to us. "I'm sorry," she said quickly. "Charlie's just upset. Our mother's death was so unexpected. It came as such a blow to both of us. He's not himself right now. I know he didn't mean what he said."

"You have no need to apologize for your brother's behavior," Rose replied. "Beatrice's death was a tragedy for all of us. With God's help, we'll get through it and come out the other side as better people."

"Yes, I hope so. Thank you." Cherise appeared to have been comforted by Rose's words. She hurried off to join her brother.

"How do you do that?" I asked Rose. "You always know just the right thing to say."

"Charlie evidently didn't think so. Aside from dropping that bombshell about the shelter, he had the nerve to all but accuse me of his mother's death."

"He can't believe that," I said.

"He doesn't have to believe it." Rose sighed. "All he needs is to have the accusation in his arsenal of ammunition to use against me."

"You sound much less confident than you did

a moment ago when you assured Cherise that things would work out and we'd all be better people in the end."

"One must always have faith in God's plan," she replied. "I shall cling to hope until someone shows up on our doorstep with a legal order to vacate the premises."

"So you're going to fight Charlie."

"I'm not fighting him, I'm fighting for what I believe in. And for what I think Beatrice would have wanted. The Gallagher House was just as much her vision as it was Peter's and mine."

"She had a meeting scheduled with you for Saturday morning. Could Beatrice have changed her mind? Do you think there's a chance that Charlie is right?"

"No," Rose said firmly. "I don't."

I wished I shared her conviction. Rose didn't give me the opportunity to voice any doubts, however. Our conversation had come to an end. Not because I was finished discussing the topic but because, having delivered her final word on the subject, Rose walked away.

Once again, I was left standing in a crowded room all by myself. It was definitely time for me to go home.

"Excuse me!"

I was halfway across the parking lot when a woman hailed me. Her heels clicked on the macadam as she hurried to catch up. I turned and waited for her. She was young, probably in her late twenties. Her long, dark hair was pulled back in a high ponytail, and her mouth had been painted in an exaggerated pout. Her shoes looked like Louboutins.

She looked vaguely familiar. Then I realized she was one of the women I'd seen at the shelter on Saturday. At the time, she'd been dressed in a T-shirt and jeans and her long hair had been hanging forward over her face. Now her manicure was new and glossy and the purse she was carrying looked like it cost more than one of my car payments.

"Can I help you?" I said.

"Hi, I'm Maribeth Abel. We haven't met, but I saw you the other day."

"At the Gallagher House."

"You do remember." She sounded pleased. "You're a friend of Rose Donovan's, right?"

"Actually, I'm Rose's niece. Melanie Travis."

I held out my hand. Maribeth's fingers were long and slender, but her grip was weaker than Kevin's.

"I didn't know Mrs. Gallagher well, but I had to come today for her service. She must have been a great lady. I know the shelter is named after her."

"Yes, it is. And despite what's happened, the Donovans will do everything in their power to ensure that the shelter will continue to operate as usual, if that's what you're worried about."

Maribeth's cheeks flushed with color. "Oh . . . No, I wasn't wondering about that at all."

I waited in silence for her to continue.

"I'm fine now. Really. I had a small problem, but it's been fixed."

I must have looked skeptical. Maribeth cast a quick look around to make sure we were alone.

"Sometimes my husband doesn't make the best decisions when he's had too much to drink," she confided. "But it doesn't happen often. And it's not his fault that I say things that get on his nerves."

I started to disagree, but Maribeth was still speaking.

"Friday night, Martin was out playing poker with his buddies and he came home in a bad mood. I told him he shouldn't bet so much if losing upset him like that. And well . . . he didn't take kindly to my criticism." She shrugged apologetically. "It was after midnight. It's not like I could call a friend at that hour. I'd heard about the shelter opening up, so I just grabbed my car keys and left."

"Good decision," I said.

"It seemed like it at the time. But Martin called the next morning and apologized profusely. He knew he'd been out of line. When I got home, he'd filled the whole downstairs with roses. That's how sorry he was."

"It sounds as though Martin needs help," I told her. "Maybe counseling. Rose's husband, Peter, can set him up with that."

"No." When Maribeth shook her head, her ponytail swung from side to side. "Martin and I are fine now. My leaving like that totally shocked him. I guess it never occurred to him that I had a choice. Martin promised it won't happen again."

I wondered if she truly believed that. We were standing close enough that I could see the dark shadows under her eyes that Maribeth had carefully camouflaged with makeup. How often did she have to tell herself that everything between her and her husband was *fine*?

"Anyway," she said, "that isn't why I wanted to talk to you."

"Oh?"

"It's about Mrs. Gallagher. We all talked about what happened."

"You mean you and the other women in the house?"

"Yes. It wouldn't have been an accident."

I was aware of that. But as far as I knew, the police hadn't released the information yet. I wondered how Maribeth knew.

"What makes you say that?" I asked.

Her chin lifted. "Because it never is," she said with a hint of defiance. "I just didn't think something like that could happen to a woman like Mrs. Gallagher. You know?"

If I had seen Maribeth walking down the street with her sleek ponytail and her Louboutins, I wouldn't have suspected something *like that* could happen to her either. Yet here we were.

"I know you were there when Rose met with that policeman," Maribeth said. "And I saw you talking to him afterward. I thought maybe you could give him a message. You know, some information?"

Now I was really curious. So it pained me to do the right thing by trying to remove myself as middleman.

"If you have information for Detective Sturgill, it would be better if you talked to him yourself. I can arrange a meeting between the two of you, if you like."

"That's not going to happen," she said firmly. "My talking to a cop would just make Martin mad all over again. And I'm not doing that. So it's you or nothing."

Me or nothing. What a lovely sentiment.

On the other hand, that meant I would get to hear Maribeth's information. So that was a win.

"In that case, I'd be happy to pass along a message."

"Tell him there was another woman in the shelter with me on Friday night. Her name was Sandra."

She had to have been the third woman I'd seen peering down at us from the shelter's second floor. My memory recalled a vague picture of medium brown hair and dark framed glasses. The rest of her image was no more than a blur.

"I got to the shelter late that night, but Sandra was still awake. Peter had left some beer in the fridge, and she and I helped ourselves. We ended up talking half the night. Sometimes it helps to share your story with someone who gets it, you know?"

I nodded.

"Sandra lives with some guy named Spencer. She said he was really pissed when she left him. He thought she'd come crawling back, but she didn't. He couldn't believe she'd been able to find another place to stay, just like that."

Which was precisely why the Gallagher House was so important.

"Sandra told me that Spencer had come around earlier in the evening. He was pounding on the door, demanding to be let in. Peter had to go outside and talk to him before he'd leave. After that, Sandra heard him yelling in the street. Spencer said no one had the right to come between him and Sandra. He was threatening to find out where the Gallaghers lived and make them sorry they'd even tried."

Chapter
Nine

Over dinner that evening, the only thing Kevin wanted to talk about was Easter. He still believed in the Easter Bunny, but having just turned six, he was old enough to start becoming suspicious.

"How does the Easter Bunny have time to go to so many houses in one night?" he wanted to know. He'd already finished his chicken and noodles. Now he was cutting his broccoli into tiny pieces and pushing it around his plate with his fork.

While we were eating, the Poodles were snoozing in various beds. Not Bud. He was under the table. If I didn't keep an eye on things, that broccoli would end up in his mouth. The little scamp would eat just about anything.

"The Easter Bunny is like Santa Claus," Davey told his brother. "Santa gets to everyone's house in one night too. It's the same thing."

"No, it's not." Kevin frowned. "Santa Claus has a sleigh. And reindeer. And they can *fly*. All the Easter Bunny can do is hop. That's not very fast."

"The Easter Bunny is a magic bunny," I said.

Sam raised a brow at that. Backing up a lie with a magical explanation wasn't the norm in our family. But I'd been stuck for an answer. And enabling Kev to believe in the wonder of the holiday for just a little longer was a good thing, wasn't it?

My younger son's eyes widened. "The Easter Bunny can do magic?"

"Umm . . . sometimes," I sputtered.

Now Sam was grinning. Apparently I couldn't count on any help from that quarter. "But only on Easter."

Kevin thought about that for a minute. "If he only has magic for one day, what does he do for the rest of the year?"

I looked at Davey. Maybe he would like to chime in again.

"He does bunny things," Davey said helpfully. Or not.

"Like what?" asked Kev.

"He eats carrots." I cast around desperately for ideas. "And weaves Easter baskets."

Sam and Davey were both staring at me now.

"I thought you bought my Easter basket at the store," Kevin said.

Evidently, not much got past this kid.

"Maybe the Easter Bunny supplies the stores with baskets," Davey told him. "You know, it's like a cottage industry."

"What's that?"

"A small business someone operates out of their own home," Sam told him. "The bunny could make the baskets in his burrow over the winter, then deliver them to stores in the spring, just in time for Easter."

Kevin popped a piece of broccoli in his mouth and chewed it slowly as he considered that. "I guess that makes sense."

Thank you, I mouthed silently to the other two members of my family.

Without their assistance, I had no idea how much longer I'd have been able to juggle Kevin's questions. And that was now, when he was six. By the time he was eight, Kev would probably be talking rings around me. Truthfully, I was kind of looking forward to that.

After dinner, the men in the family settled in the living room to watch a movie about car racing. I sat down at the kitchen table and gave Rose a call. Earlier, we'd both been sidetracked by Charlie, and I'd forgotten to tell her about

Detective Sturgill's warning. I also wanted to discuss what Maribeth had told me.

Rose picked up on the first ring. "Hello, Melanie. I was just about to call you."

"Good. Then we'll have plenty to talk about."

"You first."

I started by relating the conversation I'd had with Maribeth outside the funeral home. "Who's this guy Spencer she was talking about?" I asked at the end. "Maribeth said that he was threatening the Gallagher family."

"Spencer Markham." Aunt Rose sighed. "I'm afraid he's a piece of work. That wasn't the first time he'd been by. Mostly he's all bluster."

"It may seem that way when Peter's around," I said. "But it's unlikely Spencer is *all* bluster if his girlfriend is taking refuge in your shelter."

"I suppose you could be right," she admitted.

"That brings me to my next point." I repeated what the detective had told me earlier.

"You're a little late with that message," Rose replied tartly. "Your detective stopped by the shelter this afternoon to have a chat with me and Peter. I gather he was at Bea's celebration of life ceremony. Is that where you spoke with him?"

"Yes. And for the record, he's not *my* detective."

"I wonder why I didn't see him," Rose mused.

"I got the impression he wasn't there to be seen."

"Then he succeeded admirably. So you've already heard that Beatrice's death wasn't an accident?"

"Sturgill told me at the ceremony," I said. "With everything else that was going on, I didn't have a chance to pass along the news."

"Everything else." She snorted. "That's a polite way of putting it. Apparently Charlie Gallagher didn't think I was sufficiently impressed by his threats. Rather than waiting to see if Peter and I would accede to his demands, he has already gone ahead and informed Detective Sturgill of his suspicions."

"*Delusions* are more like it," I muttered.

Yes, I still had unanswered questions. But as far as I was concerned, Rose was innocent until proven otherwise.

"Nevertheless, Charlie told the detective that I had a very good reason for wanting his mother dead."

"But you didn't."

"That's not how Charlie tells the story. And it seems that the detective made a very receptive audience. Though he didn't say as much, I gather I am now a suspect in Beatrice's death. Detective Sturgill asked if I had an alibi for the early hours of Saturday morning."

"Do you?"

"No, unfortunately. I was asleep. By myself, in the apartment downstairs."

"But Peter . . ." I began. Then my voice dwindled away. Maybe this part was none of my business.

"He spent the night at the hospital, sitting with an old friend whose mother was dying," she replied, even though I hadn't had the nerve to ask. "So there's no one who can corroborate my story."

Sandra and Maribeth had been awake, just upstairs, for most of that night. But that wasn't much help if the three women hadn't crossed paths. I wondered if Spencer Markham—who'd been tossed off the premises only hours earlier—had an alibi for the time in question.

"Did you tell Detective Sturgill about Spencer's antics the evening before?"

"Peter did. Their confrontation took place just before he left for the hospital."

"And?"

"The detective wrote down Spencer's name, but I can't say he seemed particularly impressed by our story. I got the feeling he felt that we might be trying to throw him off the scent."

That didn't come as a surprise. Detective Sturgill was ever the skeptic when it came to information he hadn't ferreted out himself.

I wondered if he'd be more impressed with Peter's and Rose's veracity if I told him he was dealing with an ex-nun and a former priest. It might help, but then again, maybe not. These days, the Catholic Church was hardly a model of pristine behavior.

"So it's come to this," said Rose. "I need your help, Melanie."

This was the second time in less than a week she'd made that request. She sounded every bit as sure of my acquiescence this time as she'd been on the first occasion. "Peg tells me that you're a dab hand when it comes to solving other people's problems."

"I'll do what I can," I told her.

"I'll expect you to do better than that," Rose said crisply.

I tried to stifle a laugh. It was like being back in middle school all over again. Apparently a giggle slipped by.

"Do you find my predicament amusing?" she inquired.

"What's funny is you acting as if I have any choice in the matter."

"Of course you have a choice. You could have made the right decision or the wrong one. Luckily, you chose correctly."

Lucky me indeed.

"Now, listen," said Rose. "I have an idea."

Of course she did. Those words, spoken in this context, suddenly sounded familiar. All at once, Rose reminded me very much of Aunt Peg. I doubted that either woman would have appreciated the comparison.

"Go on," I said.

"Under the circumstances, I've reluctantly reached the conclusion that I might not have known Beatrice as well as I thought. Certainly, nothing in our acquaintance prepared me for the possibility that she might be targeted for murder."

"I can see that."

"Bea's best friend was a woman named Alyssa Daigle. You should go talk to her. Pick her brain, as they say. She and Beatrice had been friends for years. If there were any skeletons in Bea's closets, Alyssa will know where to find them."

That sounded promising.

I took down Alyssa Daigle's contact information and called her as soon as Rose and I had hung up. I introduced myself, mentioned that Rose had recommended that I get in touch, and asked if we could meet somewhere for coffee and a quick chat.

Alyssa—she corrected me firmly when I called her Mrs. Daigle—wasn't having that. After discovering that Rose was my aunt, she invited me to her house the following morning. "Any friend of Bea's is a friend of mine," she said happily.

I probably should have corrected her misconception. Instead I let it stand for the time being. I'd tell Alyssa the truth tomorrow, once I already had my foot in the door.

"I have an errand to run tomorrow morning," I told Sam later that night as we were getting ready for bed.

The boys were already asleep, and the dogs

were spread out among our three bedrooms, each in his or her usual spot. Faith was with us. For now, she was lying on the floor, but at some point during the night she would find her way up onto our bed. Plum was in a comfy crate in a corner of the room.

"Are you doing Easter stuff?" Sam raised his arms and pulled a long-sleeved polo shirt off over his head.

I took a moment to admire the view. "Not exactly."

He already knew all about the Gallagher House, the Easter egg hunt, and that Peter and Rose's benefactor had died under suspicious circumstances. So now it didn't take him more than a moment or two to reach the correct conclusion.

"Is Rose in trouble?"

I nodded.

"And she asked for your help?"

I nodded again. "I know it's spring break and the boys are home from school. But Davey can keep an eye on Kev when you need to work. And I really shouldn't be gone much."

"Not much?" Sam looked skeptical. As well he might. This wasn't our first time around the block.

"Hardly at all," I said. I've never been a good liar. There's a reason why I don't play poker. Well, that, and because no one ever asks me to.

"Beatrice Gallagher's son inherited the building that houses Rose and Peter's shelter, and he wants to evict them. Plus, he told the police that his mother had decided to withdraw her support, and that Rose killed her before she could do so." The words came out in a rush. Shirt in hand, Sam just stood and listened. That was another good reason to keep talking. "And Rose doesn't have an alibi."

"That does sound like trouble. I guess you'd better see what you can do."

I crossed the bedroom, stood up on my toes, and kissed him. "I love you. Even if I'm gone during the day, I'll be home every night. All night long. Just so you know."

Sam didn't need a road map to see where this was heading. His arms were already curling around my waist to pull me closer. I drew in a deep breath, appreciating the scent of his skin and how hard his body was next to mine. I snuggled against his chest.

"I'll keep that in mind," he murmured.

That's what I was hoping.

Chapter
Ten

Alyssa Daigle lived in a lovely older home on Shippan Point, a small peninsula of land that extends into Long Island Sound to form the southernmost tip of Stamford. Her house was Victorian in style with tall windows, an abundance of ornate trim, and a front porch enclosed by a decorative spindle railing.

As soon as I rang the doorbell, a dog began to bark enthusiastically. Judging by its high-pitched voice, a very small dog. I heard the sound of nails scrambling across a floor; then a woman said, "Lazlo, really. That's enough."

The door drew open seconds later. Alyssa Daigle filled the doorway.

She was a heavyset woman, probably in her

late fifties, with olive skin and dark hair that curled around her head in a halo of frizzy ringlets. Dressed in a caftan whose color scheme was flashy enough to stop traffic, Alyssa greeted me with a bright smile. When she opened her arms wide to welcome me to her home, I thought for a moment that she might smother me in a hug.

Instead she stepped back and leaned down to scoop up the slender gray and white dog who was dancing around her feet. "You must be Melanie," she said. "I hope you like dogs. This is Lazlo. Don't worry. His bark is worse than his bite."

"I'm not worried." I stepped inside and she closed the door behind me. "I love dogs. We have six."

"Six?" Her dark eyebrows flew upward. "That's like a whole kennel. I hope they're little ones."

"No, not really. Five of them are Standard Poodles."

"Those are the supersized ones, right?"

"More or less," I agreed.

Aunt Peg would have hated that description. It made the Poodles sound like a fast food order. I'd have to be sure to tell her about it.

I held out my hand for Lazlo to sniff. He had big dark eyes and a tapered tail that was smacking against Alyssa's hip as it whipped happily back and forth. The nails on the dog's delicate front paws were painted to match his owner's caftan. He touched his nose to my fingertips, then gave them a gentle lick.

"Lazlo's an Italian Greyhound," Alyssa said. "They're like an ancient breed. Did you ever see those racing dogs that run around in circles after a mechanical rabbit? Lazlo's the same kind of dog, except shrunk down so they can fit in people's houses."

I would have replied but Alyssa had already turned to walk across the travertine floor, leading the way to a living room that was stuffed with furniture. And she was still talking. "Enough about the dog already. Do you want something to drink? I made a pitcher of Bloody Marys. They're pretty spicy. I hope you like a little heat."

Unexpectedly, the question brought to mind the previous night's activities. My cheeks reddened and I nearly laughed. Alyssa didn't notice. Apparently she'd taken my lack of a reply as agreement.

She dumped Lazlo gently onto a plump couch cushion. "Have a seat. You two can get acquainted while I go and get our refreshments."

Lazlo hopped nimbly from the cushion to the top of the couch's back pillow. I sat down in a chair across from him. The elegant dog perched on the pillow in a very upright pose. He regarded me calmly, ears folded back along his sleek head, as he assumed the role of host in his mistress's absence.

"Nice to meet you, Lazlo," I said. He didn't deign to reply.

I heard the clink of ice cubes coming from the rear of the house. Bloody Marys, really? It wasn't even noon yet. If Alyssa was this talkative now, I could only imagine what she might be like after a couple of drinks.

"Here we are," she called out gaily. She reentered the room carrying a small tray.

One end of the tray held a tall pitcher. Two glasses, each with a stick of celery, were on the other. A dish contained several wedges of lime. Alyssa set the tray down on the coffee table and took a seat on the couch.

"I'll pour," she announced. "Meanwhile you can tell me why you're here."

"I want to talk to you about your friend, Beatrice."

"You already told me that on the phone."

With practiced efficiency, Alyssa filled both glasses nearly to the brim. She squeezed a lime wedge into each, before handing one to me. When she settled back on the couch, her head and shoulders were just in front of where Lazlo was sitting. The graceful dog dipped his head down to look into her glass. I hoped Alyssa wasn't planning on giving him a sip.

"So, what do you want to know?" she asked.

I'd already decided she was the kind of woman who would appreciate a direct approach. "Why someone would have wanted to kill her."

Alyssa nodded. She took a long swallow from her drink. When she lowered the glass again, there was a tomato juice moustache above her upper lip. "I'd like to know that myself. What are you, some kind of detective?"

"Some kind," I agreed. "My Aunt Rose asked for my help."

"Yeah, I can see that. She and her husband are up the creek now, aren't they? They just opened that shelter of theirs and now they're going to have to shut down again."

The first small sip of my Bloody Mary had left me gasping for breath. The second one was probably growing hair on my chest. Alyssa mixed a mean cocktail. I'd probably consumed more alcohol in the past five minutes than in the previous five months. At this rate, my hostess wasn't the only one whose tongue would be on fire.

"Beatrice's son, Charlie, told the police that Rose was mad enough at Bea to want to kill her."

"Was she?" Alyssa asked, leaning forward with interest.

"No."

"Did she?"

"No." The second time my answer was even more emphatic.

"Good thing. It'd be a shame to think a former nun would be capable of doing something like that."

"She isn't," I said firmly. "Besides, Rose had no reason to want to harm Beatrice. Not only was the woman their biggest benefactor, but she and Bea were friends."

Alyssa tipped her head to one side. Behind her, Lazlo did the same. That was pretty cute. "So what Charlie said isn't true? Bea wasn't about to pull the plug on the Gallagher House?"

"Not that Rose was aware of. Where did you hear that?"

"At Bea's ceremony. The two kids, Charlie and Cherise, were talking about it, and next thing you know, the news had traveled all around the room."

"Does it make sense to you?" I asked. "Would Beatrice have donated the house for a good cause, put her family's name on it, and then changed her mind barely more than a month later?"

Alyssa shrugged. Her glass was already three-quarters empty. She picked up the pitcher and topped it off. Meanwhile my tongue was burning. I was half-afraid there might be permanent damage. The woman must have the constitution of a bull.

"Here's the thing," she said, when she'd sat back. "Now that Bea is gone, people are talking about her like she was some kind of angel. But take it from me, she was never that. Bea was a strong woman. There were some sharp edges to her too."

"What do you mean?"

"Her husband, Howie." Alyssa peered at me

over the rim of her glass. "Did you ever meet him?"

I shook my head and chanced another small sip. Maybe the alcohol would numb the pain in my tongue.

"He was Mr. Tough Guy, that was his schtick. He wanted people's respect and he made sure he got it. When they were out in public together, Bea became the little woman. She faded into the background. It was almost like she was invisible.

"But at home? That was Bea's domain. She was the strictest mother on the block. She raised those kids to be solid citizens who knew how to do what they were told. And that was all on her. Because when Charlie and Cherise were growing up, Howie was working eighteen hours a day. Bea had to figure out how to cope, and she did."

If those children had been raised to do what their mother wanted, where had the idea to shut down the shelter come from? Now that Beatrice was gone, was this Charlie's way of rebelling against his strict upbringing?

"I never met Beatrice," I said. "I only know her through the things that you and Rose have told me. She must have been an intriguing woman."

"She certainly was," Alyssa said. She'd just topped off her drink for the second time. In her place, I'd have been floating. "Bea was always up to something. I'll tell you a little secret. She had a boyfriend."

"She did?"

Alyssa nodded. Lazlo yawned. Apparently our conversation wasn't sufficiently interesting to him.

"When did Beatrice have a boyfriend?" I asked. "When she was married?"

"Oh no, never." Alyssa waved a hand through the air. Luckily, it wasn't the one holding her glass. "Bea was devoted to Howie. Just like he was to her. No, this was after he died. Recently. Within the past year."

I frowned. "So why was it a secret?"

"She didn't want the kids to know. They wouldn't have approved."

"Why not?"

Alyssa's shoulders rose and fell in a perplexed shrug. "You know how kids are. When it comes to a parent—especially their mother—they only see one dimension. To Charlie and Cherise, Bea wasn't an attractive middle-aged woman with needs of her own. She was just their mom."

"That's too bad," I said. "Did you know him?"

"Sure, I knew him." She smiled. "Morty wasn't my type, but Bea liked him. She knew the relationship was going to cause problems, though. So she broke it off with him a couple of weeks ago."

"How did Morty feel about that?"

"He wasn't happy at all." Her words were

slightly slurred. "Morty had told Bea he was in love with her. And why wouldn't he be? Bea was a catch."

Alyssa was on a roll now. I nodded to keep her talking.

"The properties, the bank accounts, the Mercedes-Benz." Alyssa leaned closer as if confiding another secret. Her body swayed slightly as she spoke. "Everything Bea had was top notch. She even had a special dog. Not just a Greyhound, an *Italian* Greyhound."

I glanced over at Lazlo. "You mean, like your dog?"

She followed the direction of my gaze and began to giggle. "Oh yeah, there he is. That's what I meant. Lazlo."

"You're saying that Lazlo was Beatrice's dog?"

"That's right."

"Did she give him to you?"

"No, Bea would never have done that. She loved Lazlo. He was her best friend. It was after she died."

This conversation was getting harder and harder to follow. And I was pretty sure I wasn't the one with the problem. "What was?"

"Charlie and Cherise didn't want Lazlo. They said he was little, but he was still a pain in the posterior. They were going to take him to the pound. So I picked him up and brought him home with me." Alyssa turned her head and made kissing noises to the small dog. He flicked an ear in her direction, but otherwise didn't respond. "Now Lazzy and I are best friends too."

"That was a nice thing to do," I said.

"Of course it was. I'm a nice person." She paused, then frowned. "But you know who isn't a nice person?"

"No. Who?"

"Bea's ex, Morty. He was another tough guy, just like Howie." She shrugged again, this time lifting her hands in the air to emphasize her point. "What can I tell you? Bea had a type and she stuck to it. Turns out, Morty was not the kind of guy who took kindly to being dumped."

"Did Beatrice tell you that?"

"More than once," Alyssa confirmed. "Because Morty didn't want to take no for an answer. Even though she'd given him his walking papers, he kept coming back and hanging around. It made me think, I'll tell you."

"Think what?" I asked.

"When I heard that Bea had had an accident, that she'd somehow fallen down the stairs in her own house. I thought, *Damn that Morty Johnstone. I'll bet he had something to do with it.*"

Chapter
Eleven

When I got home, everyone was in the back-yard, including Aunt Peg. It looked as though the two puppies, Plum and Joker, were having the handling lesson they'd missed out on a few days earlier. Or, as Kevin liked to say, my family was playing dog show.

For a minute, I stood and watched from the driveway. Four handlers and their dogs had formed a disorderly line. Sam was in front with Plum. Her four feet were on the ground where they were supposed to be, but her pretty head was turned backward so she could see what was going on behind her.

Davey was in the second spot with his dog, Augie. A retired champion, Augie was an old hand at this. He'd already stacked himself and was waiting to see what Davey wanted him to do next. Taking his Poodle's compliance for granted, my teenage son had pulled out his phone and was staring down at the screen.

Aunt Peg was in third place with Joker. Naturally, her puppy had his head up, his tail up, and was doing just what she wanted him to do. Despite her placement in the middle of the line, she appeared to be the one issuing orders. No surprise there.

Kevin, with Bud on the end of his leash, was making a valiant attempt to bring up the rear. Tar was loose in the yard, however. The big dog had his nose down and his tail in the air as he sniffed something interesting. Bud, ever curious, was whining under his breath as he tried to drag Kev in that direction.

Faith and Eve were watching the proceedings from the deck. Both bitches looked pleased not to have been conscripted to join that motley crew. I knew just how they felt.

I was just about to go and join them when Aunt Peg called me over.

"You there!" she said, hailing me as I came through the gate. "We need a judge. Come and help out."

"You there? *Really?*" I walked in their direction. "I have a name."

"Yes, but it's bad form for exhibitors to advertise a prior relationship with the judge while they're in the show ring. I'm pretending we just met."

As if there was anyone in the entire dog show world that Aunt Peg had *just met*.

"I don't see a ring," I said.

"I don't see a ring either," Kevin piped up. He looked around as if he thought an enclosure might magically appear.

My son didn't seem to be aware that Bud's leash was now wrapped twice around his lower legs. I figured they had about ten seconds before boy and dog were both tangled in a heap on the ground. I headed that way first.

"It's metaphorical," Aunt Peg said.

"I think you mean invisible." Davey laughed. "But Mom, we really do need someone to be the judge. Otherwise there's no one to tell us what to do."

I cocked a brow in Aunt Peg's direction, but didn't voice the comment aloud. I was too busy separating Bud and Kevin into two different pieces. As soon as I'd accomplished that, Kev sat down on the ground and pulled Bud into his lap for a hug.

The judge had barely arrived on the scene and already it looked as though we'd lost a competitor.

I stood up, backed away from the line, and asked, "What have you three done so far?"

"We just got out here," Sam told me. "Start from the beginning."

"Right. Then let's get everybody settled by taking them once around. Sam, since you're in front, you get to choose how big a circle you want to make. Everyone else, follow the leader."

"Got it." Sam balled up Plum's slender leash in his hand. He gave her a reassuring pat. Poodley exuberance was a fine thing in the show ring, but now he wanted the puppy to learn how to behave.

Sam glanced back at Davey and Aunt Peg. "Is everybody ready?"

"Wait for me!" Kevin pushed Bud off his lap and jumped up. "Bud and I are coming too."

The initial attempt was all over the place. The ragtag line that wandered around our backyard in fits and starts wouldn't have passed muster in any show ring I'd ever seen. But that hardly mattered. The puppies' dog show debut was still a month away. And this was only their first lesson. Things were bound to improve from here.

With Aunt Peg in charge, I had no doubt that Joker and Plum would look like a couple of pros in no time.

Alyssa had given me Morty Johnstone's contact information before I left her house. Actually, I got the impression she was hoping that I would show up at his place of business, grab him by the ear, and march him down to the police station. Unfortunately for her, that was more Aunt Peg's style than mine.

Johnstone Plumbing Supply was located two towns over, in Norwalk. The retail store occupied a small corner in a strip mall on the Post Road. The discount shoe store next door was filled with people, but Morty's place was virtually empty. Or maybe it just looked that way because the front windows were so grimy that I could barely see inside.

A bell above the door jangled when I let myself in. The shop in front of me was crammed with rows of shelving, each stocked with an abundant selection of tools and gadgets I had no idea what to do with. I did recognize the two kitchen sinks that were leaning up against a side wall.

"Be right there," a voice called from somewhere in the back.

Following the sound, I ended up at a waist-high counter with a cash register on one end. The remainder of the surface was cluttered with a pile of chrome shower heads, a stack of posters about workplace safety, and a glass jar that was filled with Slim Jims.

A moment later a man popped his head out of the open doorway behind the counter. "You need advice, or you just want to look around?"

"That depends," I said. "Are you Morty Johnstone?"

The man smiled, like he was delighted to see

me. Maybe he didn't get many visitors. Or customers, for that matter.

"That's me. In the flesh." He stepped out of the back room, walked toward me, and braced both his hands on the counter. "What can I do you for?"

Morty probably had a few years on Beatrice, but he was still in pretty good shape. Hardly taller than I was, he had broad shoulders and muscular forearms. The sleeves of his work shirt were rolled up past his elbows, and a chunky metal watch circled his wrist. His hair was crew-cut short, and it had been a few days since his last shave.

"I'm Melanie Travis," I told him. "Alyssa Daigle recommended that I talk to you."

"Is that so?" Morty's friendly smile vanished. "What does she want now?"

"She and I are both interested in finding out what happened to Beatrice Gallagher."

"Poor Bea." His attitude softened. "She didn't deserve that."

"No, she didn't. Do you mind if I ask you a few questions?"

He gazed around the empty store. "I guess it's all right. Step behind the counter and we can talk in my office."

Morty's office turned out to be a large storage space that was filled with crates and boxes. A battered desk was pushed up against a wall. There was a single chair next to it.

Morty offered the chair to me. Then he folded his arms over his chest and leaned back against the edge of the desk. It didn't look as though he intended for this to be a long conversation.

"Shoot," he said.

"I understand that you and Beatrice were a couple until recently."

"That Alyssa." Morty snorted. "She has a big mouth."

I bit back a smile. It wasn't as though I could refute that.

"She ended your relationship, and you weren't happy about it."

"No," he corrected me. "I was the one who ended things between Bea and me."

I hadn't expected that. "Why?"

Morty shrugged. "The relationship had just run its course, I guess. She was a nice lady, but she could be bossy too. She liked to run people's lives for them. She was always telling me what to do, and giving me advice whether I wanted to hear it or not."

"That doesn't sound so terrible," I said.

"Lady, I'm sixty-one years old. If I don't know how to manage my own life by now, people should just leave me alone to make my own mistakes." Morty shook his head. "Plus, there were those two kids of hers."

"What about them?"

"They're in their twenties, for Pete's sake. But

they hardly acted like it. They were always fighting with Bea about some dumb thing or other. Whole family used words like they were daggers. It wouldn't have killed the kids to find out that their mother was boinking someone. I've never been a sneak-in-the-back-door kind of guy. It seemed silly to start now."

"You must have had your own key to Beatrice's place," I said casually.

"Yup. She gave it to me early on. I still have it, not that there's anything I need it for."

I filed that away for future reference, then shifted my body fractionally in the chair. Its hard seat made it difficult to find a comfortable position. I wondered why Morty didn't replace it with something better.

"Alyssa said you were attracted to Bea's money," I mentioned.

"So? That's not a crime. And there was certainly plenty of it. Bea, she liked to live pretty large. I didn't mind being along for the ride."

I glanced around the shabby room. "So maybe you got mad when your free ride ended?"

"Is that something else Alyssa told you?" Morty scowled. "That woman needs to learn how to mind her own business. I didn't need Bea's money. What she and I had, it was never about that."

"No?" Hadn't he just told me differently?

"Look around," Morty said.

I'd already done that. Stacks of wooden packing crates were piled all the way to the rafters. There was plenty of dust too. The whole place looked like it could use a good cleaning.

"I get it," he said. "The store doesn't look like much. But it doesn't have to. I hardly ever get walk-in customers. Most of my business comes from online and catalog sales. I'm running the biggest plumbing supply business in Connecticut out of this office."

"Really?"

Morty nodded.

"Then you ought to buy yourself a more comfortable chair."

Unexpectedly, he chuckled. He had the raspy laugh of a longtime smoker. "I know, I hate that thing too. But I've got a bad back and sitting up straight helps. So I gotta put up with it, whether I want to or not."

I stood up. I was almost ready to go. Plus, my butt was killing me.

"Beatrice didn't fall by accident," I told him. "Somebody pushed her down the stairs."

"So I heard. It wasn't me. I'm willing to swear that on a stack of Bibles."

People who felt the need to overcompensate when declaring their innocence always raised my suspicions. I mean, think about it. Why would a whole stack of Bibles be more likely to ensure the honesty of an oath than just one?

"Who do you think might have done it?" I

asked as we left his office and headed for the front of the store.

"Here's the thing about people," Morty said. "They're not always what they appear to be. Take Alyssa, for example. She and Bea knew each other for years. And despite what Alyssa might have told you, it's not like everything was always copacetic in their relationship."

"Oh?" I abruptly stopped walking.

"Not even close. There's a word for it now. Didn't even exist when those two first met, but it describes them perfectly. You ever heard of something called frenemies?"

I nodded.

"That's what they were. To hear Bea tell it, she and Alyssa spent their whole lives trying to outdo one another. Everything was a competition with those two. Husbands, card games, wallpaper . . ." Morty shook his head. "Even pets. It always mattered whose was better, and Alyssa was mostly on the losing end. That kind of thing can really irritate you after a while."

"Pets?" I said.

"Oh yeah." Monty laughed. "There was this crazy looking little dog. It was some special breed that used to belong to royalty or something. Bea got herself one and Alyssa was so jealous she was just about green."

"Are you talking about Lazlo?"

"Yeah, Lazlo. That was his name. Bea hasn't

even been gone a week and guess who has the dog now? Alyssa, that's who. I rest my case."

Morty had a case. I wished I had one too. It was hard not to envy the power of his conviction.

"You want to know who I thought was most likely to fly off the handle and do something stupid?" he asked. "My vote goes to Alyssa. Maybe she finally got tired of always being second best."

Chapter
Twelve

After I left Norwalk, I stopped at home to pick up Faith. Sam and the boys were out back working on the treehouse. I gave them a quick wave, then loaded Faith in the car and drove to downtown Stamford. The big Poodle made a great copilot. She loved having the windows open, she didn't argue about my choice of music, and every destination we arrived at was her favorite—at least for the moment.

I'd called ahead, so I knew Rose was at the Gallagher House. The Donovans' minivan wasn't parked nearby. I assumed that meant Peter was out. The parking space in front of the shelter was occupied by a shiny red Jaguar coupe that looked very much out of place in the neighborhood. I pulled my trusty, older-model Volvo in behind it.

I hopped Faith out of the passenger side of the car and snapped a slender leather leash to her collar. She sniffed at a clump of dead grass; then she glanced at the steps that led to the front door before giving me a quizzical look. Usually our car trips ended at fun destinations, like parks or dog shows. I could tell by the expression on her face that she didn't think the Gallagher House looked like much fun.

"We're going to see Aunt Rose," I told her as we walked around the house to the back entrance that led directly to Peter and Rose's apartment.

Faith woofed softly in acknowledgment. Aunt Peg's name would have been greeted with an enthusiastic yip. I suspected Faith was reminding me that Rose didn't like dogs.

"Tough cookies," I said. "You're the nicest dog I know. Anyone should be thrilled to have you come and visit."

We had to walk down several steps to get to the door. As I raised my hand to knock, I heard the sound of voices coming from inside the small apartment. Faith's ears pricked. She was listening too. Rose hadn't told me she was expecting anyone. I hoped we wouldn't be interrupting.

When she opened the door, Rose looked happy to see me. Then her gaze dropped to Faith.

"Oh," she said.

"This is Faith," I reminded her. Faith's graying muzzle made her easily distinguishable from our other black Poodles. "You've met before."

"Indeed. But I didn't expect to find her here." Briefly Rose's gaze skimmed past me. "I hope there's just one?"

"One what?" asked a voice from within the room.

I stepped inside and Faith followed me. Frowning, Rose closed the door behind us.

Cherise Gallagher was seated in the dining area. Her blond hair was pinned up in a messy bun and her face looked pale. Her fingers, tipped by nails that were short and ragged, were wrapped around a mug on the table in front of her. Cherise stared at Faith as if she'd never seen anything like her before.

"What is that?" she asked.

"A Standard Poodle," Rose replied with a sigh.

I looked at her in surprise.

"What?" she said. "You think I don't listen?"

"Rose is a great listener." Cherise peered at me sullenly. It seemed she was the one who hadn't wanted to be interrupted. "You look familiar."

"We met at your mother's celebration of life ceremony," I told her. "I was there with Rose."

She shrugged. Obviously I hadn't made much

of an impression. "That's why I'm here. I came to apologize for Charlie. He knows he was out of line."

"He does?" I said skeptically. "He seemed pretty sure of himself."

"Charlie is always sure of himself—even when he's wrong." Cherise rose from her seat and turned to Rose. "Don't feel as though you have to make any hasty decisions. I'll work on Charlie until he listens to reason. We'll be able to figure something out."

"I appreciate that." Rose gathered Cherise into her arms for a warm hug. The embrace lasted several seconds longer than I expected. Both women seemed reluctant for it to end.

"You're sure you're all right?" Rose asked as they disengaged.

"I will be." Cherise nodded. "I'll have to be, won't I? Thank you for everything."

Aunt Rose walked her to the door. "I'm here anytime you want to talk. My door is always open, you know that."

"What was that about?" I asked when Cherise had gone.

Aunt Rose picked up the mug that had been left on the table and placed it in her small sink. Then she motioned for me to take a seat. I sat down in one of the armchairs and Rose took the other. Faith lay down across my feet.

"Cherise is distraught over losing her mother. She told me that she'd barely slept or eaten since it happened. She was the one who found her, you know."

"No, I hadn't known that."

"I can only imagine how awful it would have been for her," Rose mused. "I'm happy to offer her whatever comfort I can."

"Were Cherise and her mother close?"

"Before this happened, I wouldn't necessarily have thought so. It just goes to show you that when it comes to families, you never really know what goes on behind closed doors."

Not when it came to our family. We never held things back. Our prickly emotions, hurt feelings, and difficult relationships were right out in the open for anyone to see.

My hand dropped down. I tunneled my fingers through Faith's topknot so I could scratch her head. Falling in love with a dog was so much less complicated.

"Do you think Cherise will be able to convince Charlie to change his mind?" I asked.

Aunt Rose pondered that for a minute. "I think she'll try," she said finally. "Charlie can be pretty bullheaded, however. He takes after his father."

"Were you aware that Beatrice had been seeing someone recently?"

Rose looked up. "You mean Morty?"

"Yes, Morty," I said, surprised. "I thought he was supposed to be a secret."

"Only from Beatrice's children. She was quite open about the relationship among her friends."

"Were they still together when you and Peter came back from Honduras?"

"Yes, but the relationship was coming to an end. That's probably why Bea spent so much time talking about him."

"That, and because you're a good listener," I said.

Rose smiled complacently. Even a decade out of the convent, she still couldn't bring herself to accept a compliment.

"How did you meet Morty?" she asked.

"Alyssa Daigle told me about him. She implied that Morty had gotten together with Beatrice because of her money, and he didn't entirely dispute that. She also said Morty was really upset when Bea broke it off."

"It wasn't just the money," Rose said mildly. "According to Bea, the sex was pretty good too."

"Aunt Rose!"

"What?" Her brow rose. "Does it shock you to hear that I might have learned a thing or two in ten years of marriage?"

"Frankly . . ." I blew out a dismayed breath. "Yes."

"Well, then you need to get over yourself, Melanie. I would like to think that you and I can have an adult conversation without having to moderate our words."

"Of course," I mumbled. This was going to take some getting used to.

"So Alyssa thinks Morty might have had a reason for wanting to harm Beatrice, is that what you're saying?"

"Yes. But according to Morty, Alyssa is the one who had the motive. Apparently, she and Beatrice had been rivals for years."

Rose frowned. "That complicates matters, doesn't it?"

"Yes. And speaking of complications, I was thinking I should track down Sandra's boyfriend, Spencer, and see what he has to say."

"That's a good idea," she agreed. "Spencer won't need much tracking down, however. He works for a comic book store in the mall."

Somehow it hadn't occurred to me that a man who was capable of yelling threats at the inhabitants of a women's shelter might also hold a perfectly ordinary job in a mall. I probably should have known better.

Instead of revealing my ignorance about the ways of the world, I merely said, "I didn't know there was a comic book store in the Town Center."

"Yes, it's on the fourth level. They sell new releases, vintage comics, and some apparel and collectibles too."

"You're very well informed." Once again, she'd surprised me. "Is that an interest of yours? Have you ever been there?"

"No, but Peter has. All in the line of duty, of course."

"He went to talk to Spencer too?"

"He did," Rose confirmed.

"Did it do any good?"

"It's hard to tell. Spencer hasn't been back here since the weekend, so that's something."

A shadow passed over Rose's face when she mentioned her husband. It suddenly occurred to me that I'd barely seen Peter since Rose and I had renewed our family ties. I hoped everything was all right.

"I didn't see your minivan out front when I came in," I mentioned. "What's Peter up to today?"

"Oh, you know Peter." Her light laugh sounded forced. "He's always out and about somewhere."

Actually, I didn't know Peter very well. The same family tensions that had fostered a rift between Rose and Aunt Peg had prevented me from ever spending a significant amount of time with Rose's husband.

I knew that Peter was a kind and caring man. He was someone who wanted his life to count for something. His goal was to leave the world a better place upon his death than it had been upon his arrival. But beyond the lofty sentiments that had inspired him to devote more than half his life to the priesthood, I knew very little about what occupied Peter's thoughts and deeds on an everyday level.

"I'm not as good a listener as you and Peter are," I said. "But I'll do my best. Is everything okay?"

Abruptly Rose's expression crumpled. The strict mantle of control with which she'd always shielded herself slipped away. Suddenly she looked as though she might cry.

"What do you need?" As I leaned toward Rose, Faith stood up. She walked around the table to press her warm body against my aunt's legs. "What can I do to help?"

"Peter's dealing with some health issues," she said in a small voice. "I won't bore you with details. But the reason we left Honduras is because he couldn't get the medical attention he needed there."

"Fairfield County has wonderful doctors." I spoke around the sudden lump in my throat. "Does he need a referral?"

"No, we've already done that part. Peter was seen almost as soon as we got back. Since then, his schedule has had to revolve around his various appointments. It means I've taken over running everything here, and, of course, I'm happy to do it. Anything that minimizes Peter's stress is beneficial."

"Absolutely," I agreed.

No wonder Peter had only been peripherally

involved in the problems surrounding Beatrice Gallagher's death. He had bigger issues of his own to deal with.

"The doctors have run their tests and analyzed the results. Now that they have answers, Peter should be starting treatment soon."

Rose had wrapped her arms around Faith's neck. I wondered if she even realized that she was hugging the Poodle to her.

"After that, everything will be fine," Rose said firmly. "I'm sure of it."

"I am too," I agreed. "Is there anything I can do to help in the meantime?"

"You're already doing more than enough. I'm well aware that I've allowed my problems to monopolize your spring vacation—"

"Don't worry about that for a minute," I said. "Peter's well-being comes first. Everything else will take care of itself."

"From your lips to God's ears," Rose uttered fervently.

Chapter Thirteen

The next morning, I set out for the Stamford Town Center armed with a new sense of resolve. I'd already been determined to find out who killed Beatrice Gallagher. But now it felt as though my quest to answer the questions surrounding her death had assumed a heightened sense of urgency.

The Town Center was a large, multilevel shopping mall in downtown Stamford. With more than a hundred stores to choose from, shoppers could find everything from clothing to entertainment, home décor to kids' toys and games. I parked in the garage on the third level and walked inside to discover that the entire mall had been transformed to celebrate the upcoming holiday.

Giant, brightly colored Easter eggs dangled over the center atrium on shiny satin ribbons. On the floor below was a fanciful pink-and-white bunny hutch. Children dressed in their best Easter outfits were having pictures taken with the Easter Bunny. The mall's sound system was playing "Here Comes Peter Cottontail."

It all brought a smile to my face—and reminded me that Easter was now just three days away. Once I finished talking to Spencer Markham, shopping for holiday supplies would be my second assignment of the day. The mall was a cornucopia of opportunity. I was sure I'd be able to find everything I needed to create a festive Easter celebration for my sons and for the children at the Gallagher House.

According to the mall index, Marvelous Comics and More was located on the fourth level. I took the escalator upstairs, stepped out onto the concourse, and took a look around. A larger-than-life cardboard cutout of Captain America stood outside a store not too far away. That had to be the place.

As I entered the store, my senses were assaulted by a cacophony of color and sound. Disco lights flashed across the ceiling. The floor beneath me hummed with a throbbing beat. Colorful posters, many not PG-rated, lined the walls. Racks and racks of comic books crisscrossed the room. The more valuable collectible items were displayed inside lit glass cases.

For a moment I just stood still, trying to take it all in. A man with a bushy moustache, dressed in a Superman costume, came dancing toward me across the floor. His hips swiveled and his feet skipped in time to the beat. Rings flashed on his upraised fingers.

He lowered his head close to mine before speaking. Anywhere else, the move would have felt intrusive. Here, it was the only way I'd be able to hear what he was saying.

"Can I help you find something?" he yelled in my ear.

"Yes, please. I'm looking for Spencer Markham."

Moustache-Man drew back in surprise. "Spencer?"

"That's right. Does he work here?"

"Yes. He's in the stockroom. I'll go get him for you." He stared at me curiously. "Can I tell him what this is about?"

I smiled and said, "No."

"Okay, then." He laughed. "Be right back."

It was at least three minutes before anyone reappeared from the back of the store. I browsed through a nearby rack of comic books while I waited. The prevailing theme seemed to be All Action, All the Time. Just looking at that many pictures of car chases and explosions was enough to make me tired.

Finally I glanced up and saw a man strolling toward me. He was around thirty, six feet tall and stocky. His gym-rat body was accentuated by an Avengers T-shirt that was molded across the taut muscles of his chest. The man's gaze traveled up and down my body; then his full lips drew upward in a dismissive sneer.

Spencer Markham, I presumed. We hadn't even met yet and already I didn't like him.

He stopped in front of me and crossed his beefy arms over his chest. "Are you the lady who wants to see me?"

"I am." I extended my hand. "Melanie Travis."

Spencer glanced down at my hand, then pointedly ignored it. "Do I know you?"

"Not yet."

"Maybe I don't want to know you," he said with a shrug. "You look like some kind of social worker."

Interesting guess. I wondered how many times Spencer had previously been contacted by representatives of the social services.

"I'm not," I told him. "Can we step outside for a few minutes?" Spencer didn't seem to have any problems hearing me, but my ears were ringing.

"I'm working here, you know."

"Two minutes," I said. "It's about Sandra."

"What about her?" Suddenly he was interested. "Is she all right?"

Spencer strode out the open entrance. He

crossed the wide hallway and leaned against the chrome and Plexiglas railing that formed a barrier between pedestrians and the atrium below. A glass elevator went skimming past as I joined him beside the rail.

"Sandra's fine," I told him. "At least as far as I know."

I hoped I wasn't wrong about that. But since the biggest threat to his girlfriend was probably the man standing in front of me, I figured it was a pretty safe guess.

"So then, what?" Spencer's expression hardened. "Are you with the police? If so, let me see your badge."

"I'm not with the police."

"Then why should I bother talking to you?"

"Maybe because you want to clear your name," I said.

"About what?"

"Beatrice Gallagher's death."

He didn't look surprised. I assumed that meant Detective Sturgill had already been by to see him.

"That had nothing to do with me," he scoffed.

"You were heard threatening her on Friday night," I said. "By Saturday morning, Beatrice was dead."

Spencer shook his head. "I wasn't threatening the old lady. I was just . . ."

"Just what?"

"Sometimes I lose my temper, okay? I get

started yelling and I end up saying things I don't mean. Things I might regret later."

I was betting that when Spencer lost his temper, he also *did* things he regretted later.

"That night, Friday night." He stopped and frowned. "I wasn't pissed at the Gallaghers. I was just pissed at life in general. It wasn't fair."

"What wasn't?"

"Sandra knows I love her. Okay, maybe the way I acted was wrong. But she didn't even give me a chance to apologize." He glared at me. "I *always* apologize."

Like that helped, I thought.

"Maybe it would be better if you stopped doing things you need to apologize for," I said.

"Yeah, well, life hasn't dealt me a cushy deal like some people get. People like Charlie Gallagher have everything they want just handed to them. Me, I have to work for every little crumb."

"Wait a minute," I said. "You know Charlie Gallagher?"

"Yeah. We were in school together. So what?"

I didn't know the answer to that. Indeed, so what? But that tidbit of information was interesting. It was also something I hadn't previously known. Along with the fact that Spencer seemed to harbor a deep resentment toward the Gallagher family, and it had been brewing for a while.

What were the chances that it had boiled over on Friday night when Spencer's girlfriend had run from him and found safety at the Gallagher House?

As another elevator whooshed past us, Spencer pushed himself away from the railing. "That's more than two minutes," he said. "Are we done here?"

"We're done," I told him. "Thank you."

He glared at me suspiciously. "For what?"

"For being so candid with me."

That earned me another dubious look. "Candid? What does that mean?"

"Truthful."

"Yeah, right." Spencer laughed as he left me. "Whatever, lady."

The conversation hadn't been the best job I'd ever done of talking to a potential suspect. Hopefully Detective Sturgill had had more luck with Spencer than I did. I consoled myself with a frozen yogurt from the food court on Level 7, then spent the next hour catching up on my Easter shopping. So the morning wasn't a total loss.

When I got back to my car, I gave Aunt Peg a call. "Can I stop by? I want to discuss a few things with you."

"Things pertaining to Rose?" she asked.

I decided to play it cagey. "Maybe."

Aunt Peg harrumphed under her breath. She wasn't fooled. "Are you bringing Faith with you?"

"Umm . . . no."

"Why not?"

"Because I'm at the Stamford Town Center and she's at home."

"Stop by and pick her up on your way," she commanded me. "My house feels lonely without an old dog around. I could use the company."

To be clear, she meant Faith's company, not mine.

What the heck, I thought. It wouldn't be the first time I'd used Faith to get my foot in a door.

"See you soon," I said.

Faith was delighted to be offered another car ride. That made two days in a row, and I was pretty sure she was keeping track. If I took her somewhere the next day too, she'd decide that daily car trips were our new routine. Then there'd be hell to pay if I missed a day.

"Leaving again so soon?" Sam stuck his head out his office door. The dogs had alerted everyone in the house to my arrival. So he knew I'd only been home for a few minutes—just long enough to find a hiding place for all the Easter supplies I'd bought—before telling Faith the good news. "The boys and I are going to the Maritime Aquarium this afternoon. There's a special exhibit on sharks. I thought you might want to come with us."

"Duty calls," I said. "Aunt Peg asked me to bring Faith over for a visit." Okay, that might have been fudging the truth. But only a little bit.

"Can Bud and I come with you?" Kevin came

racing down the hallway. His sock-covered feet were sliding on the hardwood floor. He skidded to a stop in front of me. "Aunt Peg wants to see Bud too."

"How do you know that?"

"She always wants to see Bud. He has spots. And dogs with spots are the best kind. Plus, she has Standard Poodles of her own she can look at, but she doesn't have any dogs like Bud."

Nobody else had a dog like Bud. As far as I'd been able to tell, the little menace was one of a kind.

"You can see Aunt Peg another time," I said. "If you come with me now, you'll miss a trip to the aquarium."

Kev bit his lip as he considered that.

"Dad's going to take you to the shark exhibit."

"*Real* sharks?" he asked.

"Swimming right in front of you."

"I choose sharks." Kevin spun around in his socks and ran away.

"That was easier than I thought it would be," I said.

"Go now before he changes his mind." Sam smiled. "And say hi to Peg for me."

"I always do. You know she likes you best."

"Not a high bar," said Sam. "Everybody likes me best."

I aimed a smack in Sam's general direction. It didn't even come close. He'd already ducked back into his office and closed the door behind him.

"He wasn't lying," I grumbled to Faith. "Everyone does like him better than me."

The big Poodle hopped up and placed her front paws on my shoulders. *Not me!* Her long pink tongue licked the underside of my chin. Faith's tail wagged happily from side to side. I closed my arms around her and gave her a hug.

Thank goodness for dogs. That's all I have to say.

Chapter
Fourteen

Aunt Peg lived in a hundred-year-old farm-house on five acres of land in back country Greenwich. For decades, she and her husband, Max, had used the acreage to house their flour-ishing family of champion Standard Poodles. Now Max was gone and so were most of the Poo-dles. I knew that the loss of fourteen-year-old Beau, earlier in the winter, had hit her particu-larly hard.

Beau's theft, years earlier, was the event that had brought Aunt Peg and me together. He was the Poodle she'd shared her thoughts with, and the one who slept on her bed at night. Beau had filled the place in Aunt Peg's heart that Faith did in mine. For that reason more than any other, I mourned his passing along with her.

When Aunt Peg opened the front door to her house, just three black Standard Poodles came racing down the steps to meet us. Joker, now the only male, led the way. Behind him were Hope, Faith's sister, and Coral, a young bitch, whom Davey had handled to her championship.

Faith hopped out of the car and politely greeted the other Poodles. They'd all known each other for years, so it only took a few moments for her to be integrated into the pack. We all trooped up the front steps together. Aunt Peg counted noses before closing the door behind us.

"I'm missing lunch to come here," I told her.

Aunt Peg was leading the way to her kitchen. Visitors she didn't care for were entertained in the living room. Friends were seated at the kitchen table and given something sweet to eat.

"Not to worry," she said. "I have cake."

Aunt Peg almost always had cake. I suspected she had a standing weekly order at the St. Moritz Bakery. I was game. Cake for lunch was better than no lunch at all.

"What kind of cake?" I asked.

"Mocha." She glanced back at me over her shoulder. "Your favorite."

Trust Aunt Peg to know that I'd be coming over, even before I'd known it myself.

If I was having cake, I'd need a cup of coffee. Aunt Peg and I had done this dance numerous times before. She didn't drink coffee. Her preferred hot beverage was Earl Grey tea. Guests who required a different drink were left to their own devices. The only concession she'd made to my frequent visits was to keep a small jar of instant coffee crystals in her pantry.

Now I walked into her kitchen, then abruptly stopped and stared. "You got a coffee maker!"

"Yes," she replied mildly. As if Jimmy Hoffa hadn't had a better chance of appearing in her kitchen than this longed-for machine.

"For me?"

Aunt Peg was cutting the strings around the bakery box on the counter. "Don't flatter yourself, Melanie. It was a gift."

"From whom?"

She slid the three layer cake slowly out of its box. "I'm surprised you don't already know. Sam gave it to me."

"He did?" He hadn't said a word to me. Fresh brewed coffee at Aunt Peg's house? I could hardly believe it. Here was yet another reason why I adored that man.

"Indeed. It came with instructions, but I haven't read them. I trust you know how to make it work?"

That would not be a problem.

Aunt Peg already had her tea in a mug on the butcher-block table. It took just minutes for my coffee to join it. In the meantime, she set out plates, napkins, and silverware. Aunt Peg also slipped each of the Poodles a large biscuit to chew on. She placed Faith's treat next to her own chair.

"Since we're skipping a meal, I shall make our first pieces extra large," Aunt Peg said after we'd both sat down.

She slid an enormous wedge of cake onto a plate and handed it to me across the table. Then she cut a large slice for herself. I took my first bite and sugary goodness filled my mouth. The mocha frosting melted on my tongue. It was heavenly.

"So?" she said as we both went back for more.

I'd debated on the way there whether I should tell Aunt Peg about Peter's illness. I'd decided it wasn't my news to share. But I saw the wistful look in Aunt Peg's eyes as she watched Faith enjoy her biscuit, and knew she was thinking about losses of her own.

As Faith stretched out and lay down in a sunny spot on the floor, I found myself blurting out, "Peter is sick."

Aunt Peg's gaze came back to me. "Yes, I know."

Why had I even hesitated? I wondered. *I should have known better.*

"That was why I found Rose and Peter a place to stay when they needed to return from Central America."

I stared at her across the table. "You told me

you did it to make sure that Rose didn't end up in your backyard."

"That too." Aunt Peg smiled.

She cut off another big bite of cake and slipped it in her mouth. I followed suit. At this rate, we'd both be back for seconds in no time.

"Why didn't you tell me?" I asked.

"I did."

"No, you didn't." I was sure of that. "When?"

"When I sent Rose to enlist your help with her Easter egg hunt. I assumed my recommending that you get involved in that ridiculous endeavor would clue you in that something was wrong."

"Well, it didn't," I grumbled.

Belatedly I realized that both of my aunts had lied to me. The two of them were more alike than they would ever want to admit.

I took another bite of cake and thought about the children at the shelter. "It isn't a ridiculous idea," I said. "And besides, you've done worse to me yourself."

"There is that," Aunt Peg agreed. She didn't sound repentant.

Luckily for her, the delicious cake was making up for a multitude of sins.

"Now that we've sorted that out," she said, "tell me how you're coming along with Rose's other problem."

Her *other problem.* As if being a suspect in a

murder investigation was no more than a minor inconvenience. Of course Aunt Peg wasn't worried. Considering her opinion of her sister-in-law, she might be rooting for the other side.

It took me less than ten minutes to sum up everything I knew. It wasn't as though I'd learned much. It would have taken me even less time if Aunt Peg hadn't placed another piece on my plate and I hadn't kept pausing to nibble on it.

"I don't know any of these people," she complained at the end. "Except, of course, for Rose. Are you sure she doesn't make a viable suspect?"

"Positive," I said.

She muttered something uncomplimentary under her breath. I just kept nibbling. After a minute, even that drew her ire.

"For pity's sake, Melanie. Stop eating like a rabbit. At this rate, we'll never get to our third slices."

One could only hope.

"Spencer Markham appears to have a grudge against the Gallagher family," she said thoughtfully. "What's that about?"

"He didn't say."

"Did you *ask*?"

Now that she mentioned it, umm . . . no.

"I assumed that most of his ranting had to do with the shelter acting as a refuge for his girlfriend, rather than the Gallaghers themselves.

Although it turns out that he's acquainted with Charlie."

"Yet another quasi-villain in your scenario." Aunt Peg nodded. "Do you suppose he was impatient enough to get his hands on his mother's money that he decided to hurry things along?"

"Possibly. He was certainly eager to claim ownership of her assets, even before they were officially his. I barely know Charlie Gallagher, but from what little I've seen, I don't like him much."

"He doesn't sound like a likable character," Aunt Peg agreed. "What about the sister?"

"Cherise was devastated by their mother's death. To all appearances, much more so than Charlie. Although maybe she's just better at expressing her emotions."

"Did the children—and I use the word loosely—live with their mother?"

"No. Rose mentioned something about the two of them sharing an apartment in Stamford."

"So presumably Beatrice should have been home alone when the fall occurred?"

"I guess so."

"Middle of the night . . ." Aunt Peg prompted. "The doors would have been locked . . . Do you see where I'm going with this?"

All at once, I did. "You're wondering who else had access to the house."

"Aren't you?" she asked dryly.

I should have been, I realized.

"Detective Sturgill didn't say anything about a break-in," I said, thinking back. "I bet Charlie and Cherise both have keys to the house. And Bea's ex-boyfriend, Morty, mentioned having one."

"What about the best friend who ended up with Beatrice's dog?" Aunt Peg said. "If she was the kind of person who'd stop by to water the plants when Beatrice was out of town, she could have one too."

Somehow I couldn't picture Alyssa puttering around Beatrice's home with a watering can. Even so, I wasn't about to discount her.

"And Rose," I said unhappily.

Aunt Peg's brow lifted.

"Well, Peter, actually. He and Beatrice were old friends. She gave him a key at some point."

"Why?"

Once again, I didn't know. That was the problem with talking to Aunt Peg. She was apt to raise more questions than she answered. Unless we were talking about dogs, in which case her opinions were many and varied—and all of them were to be accepted as gospel truth.

"I suppose that doesn't matter now," she mused. "As long as you're sure about Rose's innocence."

"I am," I muttered. Yet again.

We both paused to eat more cake.

"Wait a minute," I said suddenly. "Maybe we're looking at this wrong. Maybe whoever killed Beatrice didn't have a key to the house. Maybe she let them in."

"In the middle of the night?"

"How do we know that the person didn't arrive earlier? All we have is an approximate time of death. We don't know what preceded that event."

"I disagree," Aunt Peg argued. "It seems to me we have a pretty fair idea about that."

"We do?"

"We know that someone entered Beatrice Gallagher's house that night. There was some sort of dispute between them. It was probably unexpected, but definitely antagonistic in nature. Because when that person left the house, Beatrice was dead."

"Why unexpected?" I asked.

"Think about it, Melanie. Shoving Beatrice down a flight of stairs was a violent—and in this case, deadly—act. But it doesn't scream premeditation to me. I'd guess it was more a crime of convenience."

Faith stood up and stretched. She glanced my way briefly to check in. A look passed between us; then Faith leaned over and placed her head in Aunt Peg's lap.

Immediately Aunt Peg put down her fork so she could stroke Faith's muzzle with her hand.

The Poodle closed her eyes and leaned into the caress. The two of them looked very pleased with themselves.

Aunt Peg has always thought better when she had her hands on a dog. Now she said abruptly, "What do you know about Beatrice's neighbors?"

"Nothing," I admitted.

"Are they old? Young? Gainfully employed? World travelers or people who sleep at home in their own beds every night?"

"Still nothing," I said.

"You should find out. We may not be sure when Beatrice's killer arrived at her house, or how he or she got inside. However, we may be reasonably certain that the guilty party left at an odd hour of the night. And very probably in a hurry."

"You're right," I realized.

"Of course I'm right. For all you know, one of her neighbors might be a night owl. Or a light sleeper. Or someone with a tricky bladder."

Hopefully not the latter, I thought. *For their sakes.*

"Someone might have seen something," I said.

Aunt Peg smirked. "It took you long enough to think of that."

Chapter
Fifteen

Beatrice's most recent home was a big step up from the first house she and her husband had shared. The three-story brick building had a handsome façade, with white trim, glossy black shutters, and a front door to match. It was located in a quiet, affluent neighborhood where stately houses sat side by side, separated only by small gardens and driveways. The whole area was peaceful and lovely.

I'd come directly from Aunt Peg's house, so Faith was in the Volvo with me. When I got out of the car, she stood up on the backseat, wagging her tail expectantly.

"I'm sorry," I said as I cracked all four car windows. "You can't come with me."

Yes, I can! I'll be good.

"I know that, but I'll be asking people to open their doors and answer my questions. It might be easier without a big black dog at my side."

I'm adorable. They'll love me.

I couldn't argue with that. Instead I said, "It's fifty degrees out. You'll be comfortable here. Take a nap until I get back."

I started with the house directly across the street. I'd noticed someone looking out a front window while I was talking to Faith, and it seemed like a good idea to begin my quest with someone who was curious. And who also kept tabs on what was happening in the neighborhood.

My first knock at the door went unanswered, however. So did the second. I knew someone was inside. So instead of knocking again, I placed my mouth close to the door and said, "I'm not selling anything."

There was a pause, then a muffled voice came back. "What do you want?"

"I want to talk to you about your neighbor, Beatrice Gallagher."

"I don't talk to the press."

"I'm not a reporter."

"I don't believe you. Go away."

So much for curiosity.

The people who lived to the right of the Gallaghers' house weren't home. Either that, or they'd also checked me out as I approached, and declined to open their door. I got the same result at the house beyond that one. As quests went, this was beginning to look like it would be a short one.

I turned around and walked back down the empty sidewalk, passing in front of the Gallaghers' house again. Now I was zero for three. I decided to give it one more try. Beatrice's immediate neighbors would have had the best chance of seeing something. There probably wasn't much point in looking farther afield than that.

As I approached the neighboring house on the other side, I heard a loud clatter coming from behind it. An annoyed screech followed. Whoever was there wasn't happy—and they were in the backyard. That was a stroke of luck. Someone who was already outside couldn't refuse to open a door.

I hurried down the driveway that ran between the two homes. Striding around the back corner of the house, I saw a middle-aged woman wearing blue jeans and sneakers. She was standing with her hands on her hips and scowling at an overturned garbage can. A ripped trash bag was on the ground beside it.

"Hello," I said. "Can I help?"

She glanced over at me and laughed. "You're kidding, right?"

I shrugged. "That doesn't look too bad. Between us, we can get it cleaned up in no time."

The woman was still skeptical. "I get paid to handle other people's garbage. What's your excuse?"

Honesty seemed like the best idea. "I was hoping to get some answers, and nobody else on the block will talk to me."

"You must be a reporter, then."

"Nope. I'm just trying to help out my aunt."

"Who's your aunt?"

"A friend of the Gallagher family."

While she thought about that, I crossed the small distance between us and righted the metal trash can. Then I grabbed one end of the torn plastic bag. The woman leaned down and picked up the other end. Juggling it between us, we were able to maneuver it into the can without spilling any of its contents. She picked up the lid and jammed it on top, then we each took a handle. Together, we hefted the garbage can back beside the wall.

"At least you're not afraid to get your hands dirty," she said. "I'm Linda."

"Melanie," I replied. "Is this your house?"

"No way." She laughed again. "This is the house I clean on Mondays, Wednesdays, and Fridays. Tuesdays, Thursdays, and Saturdays, I'm across town. So whatever kind of information you're looking for, I won't be much help."

Great. It looked as though I'd struck out again.

"Did you know Beatrice Gallagher?" I asked.

"Sure. She invited me and the queen to tea most afternoons."

"I'm guessing that's a no."

"Good guess." Linda shaded her eyes from the sun and stared at me. "Anything else?"

I shook my head.

"Thanks for the help." Linda started toward the back steps. Then she paused. "Okay. I didn't know Mrs. Gallagher. But I did meet her once or twice. She seemed like a nice lady."

"That's what I've heard." I was already turning to leave.

"Not everyone thought so."

And I turned back. "No?"

"Her kids stopped by sometimes. Two of them. They were a pouty pair. It wasn't happy times when they were around."

"How do you know that?"

"It didn't take a genius to figure it out. There'd be yelling and slamming doors. Typical teenage tantrums. Except these kids weren't teenagers."

"Did you hear what the yelling was about?"

"Nope. Didn't try to either. None of my business." Linda was done talking. She skipped up the steps and went inside.

Well this idea had been a bust. At least Faith was waiting for me back in my car. That was enough to bring a smile to my face.

Retracing my steps down the driveway, I'd almost reached the sidewalk before I noticed a man standing in front of the Gallaghers' house. He was wearing a worn leather jacket with a Burberry scarf wrapped around his neck. When he glanced my way, I blinked in surprise. It was Charlie Gallagher.

As soon as he saw me, Charlie's face hardened into a scowl. He strode toward me, shoulder tipped forward pugnaciously. I stopped and waited for him.

"This is private property," Charlie snapped. "What are you doing sneaking around behind my house?" Then he peered at me more closely. "I know you."

"Yes, we met at your mother's ceremony. And I wasn't on your property. I was talking to your neighbor's cleaning lady."

"Oh yeah? About what?"

I thought about simply pushing past him. My car was no more than a dozen feet away. I could see Faith standing on the front seat with her nose wedged in the small space that was open at the top of the window. But after the way Charlie had treated Rose the other day, I'd just about had it with his entitled attitude.

"We were talking about you and your sister," I said. "And how often you came over here to fight with your mother."

Charlie reared back in surprise. "That wasn't me."

I'd just met Linda, but I had no reason to doubt what she'd told me. And I had more than enough reasons to doubt Charlie. On the other hand, Linda could have been wrong about what she'd heard.

"Who was it, then?" I asked.

Charlie glanced over his shoulder. A black Jeep was parked in the driveway on the other side of the Gallaghers' house. There was another man standing beside it. I doubted he could hear what we were saying, but he was watching our interaction from afar.

"That would have been Cherise," Charlie muttered. He didn't sound happy. "And her fiancé."

Now I was the one who looked surprised. "Cherise is engaged?"

"Not anymore." He waved his friend over. "Scott knows more about that than I do. He's her ex."

I processed that more slowly than I should have. Apparently the efficacy of my brain cells was impeded by Scott's approach. The man was tall and mouthwateringly handsome, with dark, wavy hair, an athletic build, and a great smile. This Adonis had been Cherise's fiancé?

I wondered who had broken up with whom. And what had induced her to let him go.

"What's going on?" Scott asked.

Charlie nudged a shoulder my way. "This is a

friend of my mother's. She was asking about Cherise."

"What about her?"

"Umm . . ."

I hadn't been struck dumb by his looks. I just didn't have anything to say. I wasn't asking about Cherise in particular. I'd been fishing around for whatever information I could get. And now, suddenly, I felt as though I'd been handed a boatload.

"So," I said, "you and Cherise."

"Yeah, I guess." Scott lifted a hand and scratched his head. "For a while anyway. Until Mrs. Gallagher got involved."

"That was a problem?"

"You could say so." He turned to Charlie. "So, are we going inside, or what?"

Charlie nodded and the two men walked away together. After they'd disappeared inside the house, I returned to my car.

Faith was waiting for me with a wagging tail and a big grin on her face. As soon as I opened the door, she jumped into my arms. Fifty pounds of flying Poodle was a lot, but I was used to her friendly assaults. I rubbed the top of her head fondly, then put her back inside. Faith went to the backseat and I climbed in front.

As I fastened my seat belt, I was still thinking about my encounter with Charlie and Scott. "Was it just me or was that weird?" I asked her.

"Woof!" Faith replied.

It was nice to have someone agree with me for a change.

My next stop was at the Stamford Police Station. The way my day had been going so far, you'd think I might have known better. But having accomplished so little in my attempt to clear Aunt Rose of suspicion, I was anxious to know whether Detective Sturgill was having more success.

The Stamford PD had moved into a new, larger building since the last time I'd visited. This wide brick structure had more windows and taller columns. Its airy entrance was supposed to be welcoming. That didn't help. I still felt intimidated as soon as I walked through the door.

Once again, Faith had to stay behind in the car. Only working and service dogs were allowed inside. This time she knew what to expect when I parked and opened the windows. Faith looked resigned as she lay down and rested her head between her paws.

"I won't be long," I promised her.

When I talked to Detective Sturgill, I never was.

I gave my name to the officer behind the reception desk, then took a seat. I knew from experience that the detective would keep me waiting. A full ten minutes passed before he appeared. By then, I was beginning to think I might have lied to Faith. I hate it when that happens.

"Ms. Travis?" Sturgill's stride was unhurried as he approached. I started to rise from my seat, but he waved me back down, then lowered his sturdy frame onto the chair beside me. "We can talk here."

Okay. So maybe Faith wouldn't be disappointed in me.

"I assume this is about Beatrice Gallagher?"

I nodded. "What have you found out?"

"You know I'm not going to answer that question."

Sure, I thought. *But it had been worth a try.*

"Is there something you want me to know?" he asked.

"Rose Donovan is innocent."

"I think so too," Sturgill said. Apparently, this was my day for surprises. "But in the absence of other viable suspects, she's still a person of interest."

"What about Spencer Markham?" I asked.

"What about him?"

"He was heard threatening the Gallagher family, just hours before Beatrice died."

"After that, he went and joined a few buddies of his at a nearby bar."

I frowned. "They vouched for his whereabouts?"

"Yup."

"And you believe them?"

A look of annoyance flitted across his face. "Let's just say, I haven't proven differently."

"Cherise Gallagher had been fighting a lot with her mother recently."

Sturgill leaned back in his chair. I was pretty sure I heard it creak. "Who told you that?"

"Her brother."

"Charlie?"

"Does she have any other brothers?"

"None that I'm aware of, Ms. Travis. What made Charlie decide to discuss his family's squabbles with you?"

"Umm . . . because I asked him if he was the cause of them," I admitted.

"So he put the blame on his sister," Sturgill said skeptically. "Do you have any siblings?"

I nodded.

"Sound familiar?"

I bit my lip and remained mum. This is why Detective Sturgill and I aren't on a first-name basis.

"Beatrice's ex-boyfriend has a key to her house," I said.

He stopped just short of shaking his head. "Are you supposed to be helping me here, or what?"

Unfortunately, the short answer to that probably would have been "or what."

The detective braced his hands on his knees and stood up. He'd already taken several steps before he glanced back at me over his shoulder. "Have a nice day, Ms. Travis."

I saw myself out. At least my dog would be happy to see me.

Chapter
Sixteen

That night after dinner, I cleared off the kitchen table and got out all the supplies we'd need to color Easter eggs. Thirty-six for the Easter egg hunt at the shelter, and another dozen for Kevin and Davey to find on Easter morning at home. Sam had already hard-boiled all the eggs we'd need earlier in the day. Even so, this was going to be a project.

"I'm in charge," Kevin said importantly. After I'd covered the tabletop with newspaper, he slid into the seat closest to the two big bowls of eggs.

"Says who?" asked Davey.

"Me," Kev informed him. "You can help."

"Gee, thanks." Davey took a seat across from him.

Curious about the proceedings, Augie came over to check things out. Reaching the table, he lifted his head and took a sniff. Unfortunately, the big Poodle was standing near the open bottle of vinegar. His lips curled in disgust as he jerked his head away.

"Sorry about that." I gave the poor dog a pat. "But you should have asked first."

"Yeah," Kevin echoed. "You should have asked first. Because that stuff *stinks*." He looked up at me. "Who's going to want to eat eggs that smell like that?"

"Don't worry. They won't smell by the time we're finished." Carefully I added a few drops of vinegar to each of the dozen bowls of colored water that were lined up across the table. We also had sheets of decals, wax crayons, and colored markers.

Kev sat up to check out his choices. "I'm going to dye all my eggs blue," he decided.

"Mine will be multicolored," Davey said.

His brother stared at him suspiciously. "What does that mean?"

"More than one color on each egg."

"I want that too!"

Of course he would, I thought. Well, Davey could help him with that part.

I put a dozen hard boiled eggs in front of each of the boys. "This should be enough to get you started. You can color or decorate them any way you like."

Kevin frowned as he surveyed the distribution of eggs. "That's not fair. You have twice as many as we do."

"When you finish the ones in front of you, you can have more," I told him. "You know I'm helping Aunt Rose with an Easter egg hunt for the kids at her shelter. So, all together, we have nearly fifty eggs to color. There will be plenty of chances for you to experiment."

"How come the Easter Bunny isn't hiding the eggs at the shelter, like he does with ours?" Kev asked.

"This time of year, he's a very busy bunny," Davey said seriously. "Sometimes adults have to help out."

"I like helping." Kev picked up an egg and plunged it into a bowl of blue dye. Liquid sloshed over the side as the egg sank to the bottom of the bowl. It was a good thing I'd lined the table with paper. "That means more eggs for us to color."

"The child at the shelter who finds the most eggs will get a bunny for a prize," I said as I fitted my first egg into the dipper.

"A real live bunny?" Kevin's eyes opened wide. "I want a bunny too!"

I really should have seen that coming.

"You have Bud," I said.

"Yeah." Davey grinned. "You don't want a bunny. Bud would eat it."

"Ewww." Kev grimaced. "That's gross."

I looked at both my sons and sighed. At what age was this parenting thing supposed to start getting easier?

Now that I'd met Scott and heard about Cherise's broken engagement, I wanted to learn more. Immediately I thought of Alyssa Daigle. Not only had the woman been Beatrice's best friend, but the first time we met, she'd talked nonstop. That made her the perfect person to answer my questions.

Last time, I hadn't known the right things to ask. This time I would do better.

Alyssa sounded happy to hear from me when I called. Especially since I started the conversation by telling her that I mixed a mean margarita and that I'd bring all the ingredients with me when I dropped by. Two seconds later, she'd invited me to lunch.

Sam stood in the kitchen and watched me assemble my go bag. I had bottles of tequila and Cointreau lined up on the counter, along with a couple of fresh limes and a shaker of salt.

"Should I ask?" he said.

"Probably not." At this point, explanations would just slow me down. "If it's any reassurance, most of this isn't for me."

"I'm not sure that helps."

I glanced at him over my shoulder. "Do we own a cocktail shaker?"

"Possibly." Sam disappeared into the dining room. I heard him rummaging around in a cabinet. A minute later, he returned with the chrome cylinder held aloft.

"Where'd you find that?"

"Tucked away behind a lot of other junk that we almost never use." Sam peered at it dubiously. "It must have been a wedding present."

That would have been eight years ago. We hadn't needed a cocktail shaker since. I took it from him and put it in the bag.

"I'm going to assume you don't need the don't drink and drive lecture," Sam said.

"Good choice."

He followed me to the door anyway. "Be careful out there."

"Always," I told him.

Once again, Alyssa greeted me with open arms. Even Lazlo seemed delighted to see me. The Italian Greyhound jitterbugged in place until I leaned down and patted his silky smooth head, then he spun around and went racing into the living room.

"I didn't expect to see you again so soon," Alyssa said. Today her voluminous caftan was covered with pink and purple stripes. "You must have missed me. I grilled some chicken. I hope you like Caesar salad. Open your bag. Let's see what's in there."

I unzipped the top and her fingers picked delicately through my contribution to our get-together. The only things she'd need to supply were ice and a couple of glasses. Alyssa nodded in satisfaction.

Minutes later, she and I were sitting at a small, round table in a sunny dining nook beside her kitchen. We each had a generous helping of chicken and salad in front of us. Beside our plates were two frosty, salt-rimmed glasses. Both were filled to the top, and there was a pitcher with premixed margaritas between us.

Lazlo came trotting over to the table. He sat down beside Alyssa and looked up at her expectantly. "I hate it when dogs beg at the table," she said, even as she cut off a small piece of chicken and lowered her hand to his mouth. The IG gobbled down the tidbit.

"Lazlo begs because you feed him."

She shook her head. "You have that backwards. If he didn't beg, I wouldn't feed him."

Whatever, I thought.

"Last time we spoke, you didn't say much about Beatrice's children," I said.

Busy eating, Alyssa paused to look up. "What about them?"

"I didn't realize that Cherise had recently been engaged."

"Yeah." She took a sip of her margarita. It must have passed muster because she quickly took another. "That was a mess."

"How come?"

"Bea didn't approve of Cherise's beau." Alyssa thought for a moment. "Scott Carr, that was his name. Seemed like a nice enough kid to me. I could see what Cherise liked about him. Scott was a real hottie. Given half a chance, I'd have climbed that body of his like a magic beanstalk."

I choked on a piece of chicken, then made a grab for my drink. The glass's salted rim made my lips sting, but the margarita tasted great going down.

"I told you about how strict Bea was, right?"

"You did." I nodded.

"She made a lot of rules. And she expected her kids to follow each one to the letter. Getting engaged to some guy Bea barely knew was definitely outside the rules. She had a fit when she found out about it."

"Maybe she'd have liked Scott better once she got to know him."

"Maybe," Alyssa allowed. "But that didn't happen. Instead Bea told Cherise to call off the engagement. Cherise refused. That turned into a fight and a half, let me tell you."

"Why didn't Beatrice approve of Scott?"

"She thought he was just a kid who didn't have much on the ball. He never finished community college and he works at some dinky job." Alyssa shrugged as if to say, *Who cares about that*? She was probably still imagining that magic beanstalk. "Howie was an overachiever. That's the kind of man Bea respected. That was what she wanted for her daughter."

"What did Cherise want?" I asked.

Alyssa speared a piece of lettuce and put it in her mouth. "She only wanted Scott. That girl had stars in her eyes. She was sure he was the love of her life. She didn't care that Scott was as poor as a gutter rat. She figured everything would work out after they were married."

"And maybe she was counting on some financial help from her mother?"

"You got that right." She refilled her glass and took a long swallow. Apparently, all this talking was thirsty work. "Have you ever seen Cherise's car?"

I pictured the red Jaguar that was parked in front of the shelter on the day when she'd been visiting Rose. "I think so."

"Then maybe you can understand how naïve Cherise is about money. She has no idea how to live without it because it's just always been there. Cherise's idea of being poor is picking out two Kate Spade purses and only buying one of them."

Alyssa burst out in a raucous laugh. After a second, I joined in. Lazlo jumped up from his spot on the floor. He landed gracefully in Alyssa's lap, and she rewarded him with another piece of chicken. At this rate, the dog would never learn any manners.

"So, what happened?" I asked. "I know the engagement ended. Did Cherise break up with Scott because Beatrice told her to?"

"No way." Alyssa shook her head emphatically. "Cherise would never have done that. She had this romantic idea that she and Scott were going to run off together. Like Romeo and Juliet. You know?"

Except presumably with a happier ending, I thought.

"Then out of the blue, Scott ended things. He even asked for his puny little ring back."

"Do you know why?" I asked.

Alyssa stopped eating to look at me across the table. "Do you want to hear Bea's version or Cherise's?"

"Both."

"According to Bea, Scott lost interest in Cherise once he found out she wasn't going to be the golden goose he'd expected to marry."

"Okay." I could see that. "And according to Cherise?"

"She said her mother had driven Scott away with all her arguing, carrying on, and acting like a crazy woman. Cherise told Bea that she'd ruined her life."

"What do you think?" I said. "Was the truth somewhere in the middle?"

Alyssa issued a small snort. "Oh no. The truth was somewhere else entirely."

"What do you mean?"

She swayed toward me over the table, her movements less steady now that she'd finished her second margarita. "Bea made me promise I wouldn't tell anyone this. But since she's gone, I guess it doesn't matter now."

"I'm sure it doesn't," I agreed readily.

"Bea was every bit as stubborn as her daughter. The two of them were both used to getting everything they wanted, and neither one was going to give in. Who knows how long the impasse between them would have gone on if Bea hadn't taken matters into her own hands and ended it."

"How did she do that?"

"Bea arranged a private meeting with Scott. She told him Howie wasn't the only one who'd had connections in the construction business. So either he could drop out of her daughter's life, or Bea would get someone to come and rearrange that pretty face of his."

"Yikes," I said.

"I know." Alyssa giggled behind her hand. "Pretty crazy, huh? But it did the trick."

Chapter
Seventeen

By the time I left Alyssa's house, it was nearly two o'clock.

She had given me plenty to think about. The first thing I wanted to do was discuss what I'd learned with Aunt Rose. She and Beatrice had also been good friends. I wondered if Rose was aware of the lengths to which Beatrice had gone to break up her daughter's engagement—and whether there'd been repercussions resulting from her actions.

It took just ten minutes to drive across town to the Gallagher House. Along the way, it occurred to me that today was Good Friday, one of the most somber days in the Catholic calendar. I was sure Peter and Rose would have attended mass earlier, but they should be home by now. Hopefully my visit wouldn't intrude upon their observance of the day.

The Donovans' silver minivan was in front of the shelter. I parked my Volvo behind it and walked around the building. I'd almost reached the steps that led to the apartment when its door opened.

Aunt Rose looked up at me quizzically. "I didn't expect to see you today. Is everything all right?"

"Maybe."

"That doesn't sound good. You'd better come in and tell us about it." She motioned me inside, then closed the door behind us.

Peter was sitting in one of the armchairs. An open Bible was cradled in his sturdy hands. He closed the book and set it aside when I entered the room.

"I'm sorry," I said. "I know it's Good Friday. Would it be better if I came back another time?"

"Our missions in other parts of the world have taught us to be flexible about religious observances when the need arises. I'm sure whatever brought you here must be important." Peter stood up, came around the table, and gathered me in a hug.

Despite being family, Rose and I still struggled to truly connect. But I'd always been drawn to Peter. The open, warmhearted man had devoted his life to making people feel better about themselves. I invariably felt comforted by his presence.

Discreetly I searched for signs that he wasn't feeling well, a circumstance that would definitely make me reschedule my visit. Thankfully, Peter appeared fine. Since Rose had discussed his health with me in confidence, I opted to respect his privacy by not bringing it up.

"I heard you'd been doing some investigating on our behalf," Peter said. "Tell us what you've found out."

I pulled off my jacket and hung it on a coat-rack in the corner. Rose dragged over another chair from the kitchen table. We all sat down.

"Investigating is a strong word for what I do," I told him. "But I have been talking to people and asking questions. Recently I've been hearing more about Beatrice's children, Cherise and Charlie. It sounds as though they both had troubled relationships with their mother."

Neither Peter nor Rose replied. A minute passed. It felt like a long time as I sat and waited them out.

"There was definitely some resentment there," Rose said finally. She spoke slowly, as if measuring her words. "It built up over the years."

"What was it caused by?"

"Bea wasn't always the most attentive mother to those kids," Peter replied. "Sometimes she let them run wild. Other times, she'd overcompensate by reining them in too hard."

I remembered Rose telling me that Peter and Beatrice had worked together years earlier when he'd been affiliated with the Stamford Community Center. Charlie and Cherise would have been teenagers then.

"One thing you should understand," he said, "is that when Bea's husband was alive, most of her time and attention was devoted to keeping him happy."

"For all the good it did her," Rose muttered under her breath.

A look passed between them. I recognized that look. I'd shared it with Sam on occasion and I knew what it meant. Peter and Rose were concealing something. Something they weren't sure they wanted to divulge.

"Tell me," I said firmly.

They both remained silent.

I turned to Rose with a hard stare. "You asked for my help. How do you expect me to do that if I don't have all the facts?"

"Peter is bound by an oath of confidentiality, due to his position."

"But you're not," I countered. "Tell me what you're thinking."

Aunt Rose sighed. "Beatrice confided in me at a particularly low time in her life. We never spoke again about what she shared with me on that occasion. Bea was a victim of domestic violence herself. That was why sponsoring the Gallagher House was so important to her."

Surprised, I rocked back in my seat. "Who was her abuser?" I asked after a moment. "Was it her husband or one of the kids?"

"It was Howie." Now that the secret was out in the open, Peter felt he could weigh in. "The problem was ongoing throughout most of their marriage. I tried several times to get him to come for counseling, but he always refused."

Peter frowned. "Eventually I advised Beatrice to leave him. But even after she'd accepted that things wouldn't change between them unless she made changes herself, Bea chose to stay. It was partly for the sake of the children, and partly because her comfortable lifestyle was important to her too. I didn't approve of the choice she made, but it was her decision. After that, all I could do was be there for her."

"I'm not sure I see how remaining with an abusive husband would have helped her family," I said.

"It didn't," Rose retorted. "Bea was kidding herself about that. Those two kids grew up knowing what kind of man their father was. They watched what was happening. They saw what she put up with over the years."

Peter nodded. "As they got older, Charlie and Cherise told her to fight back. They hated that she never did."

I could only imagine how they'd felt. Helpless to intervene themselves, the pair must have been constantly stressed.

"The way they grew up made them lose all re-spect for Beatrice," Rose added. "By the time they were teenagers, Charlie and Cherise were questioning every decision Beatrice made, and every rule she tried to enforce. The stricter she tried to be, the more they rebelled."

"That sounds utterly miserable for all of them," I said.

Peter nodded. "Beatrice held the purse strings. She thought she could control them that way. In-stead it had the opposite effect. Charlie and Cherise both resented that she was giving money away to charity while being stingy with them."

Having seen the pair's vehicles, it seemed that *stingy* was a relative term. Then I followed Peter's line of thought, and realized something else.

"Is that why Charlie was so awful to you at Beatrice's ceremony?" I said to Rose.

"Yes, indeed. He's obviously eager to claw this place back into the family coffers as soon as he can."

"And yet Cherise appears to be on your side."

Rose shrugged. "I've wondered about that myself. Perhaps she has more sympathy for what we're doing here because she's a woman."

Or maybe Cherise had something to feel guilty about, I thought. And her goodwill toward the shelter was an attempt to make amends.

"What do you know about her engagement?" I asked.

"I know that Beatrice wasn't in favor of the young man. She threatened to disinherit Cherise if she didn't call it off."

"That's not all she threatened to do," I said darkly.

Peter and Rose both looked at me with interest.

"According to Alyssa, Beatrice told Scott that if he didn't leave Cherise alone, she would have someone beat him up. *Rearrange his pretty face* were the words that she used."

"No." Rose exhaled sharply. "Bea would never have done such a thing."

"She might have threatened to, though," Peter said, considering the idea. "Sad to say, Bea was no stranger to violence. Maybe she thought she would use it to further her own ends for once."

"That's outrageous!" Rose cried.

"Doesn't mean it isn't true." Peter was ever the voice of reason.

"Did Cherise know about that?" Rose asked me.

"I don't know. Alyssa didn't say. But the result was that Scott broke the engagement and asked for his ring back."

"Under duress," Rose muttered.

"However it came about, Beatrice was responsible for Cherise being dumped by a man she thought was the love of her life."

Peter leaned back in his seat. He leaned his elbows on the chair's plump arms and steepled his fingers in front of his face. "Kids who grow up in homes that are broken like that often have issues that follow them throughout their whole lives. They've seen how brutality can make an impact. And maybe they begin to think it's a tool that can work for them too."

Was he saying what I thought he was saying?

Rose and I both started to speak at once. Peter held up a hand to quiet us.

"I'm not trying to point a finger here. I'm only saying that a wise person would keep an open mind about the possibility . . ."

"That Cherise lost her temper and pushed her mother down the stairs," I quietly finished the sentence for him.

Rose looked stunned. Her hand flew up to cover her heart. I heard her suck in a breath and hold it, as if that could somehow turn back time and erase what had been said.

"The way those kids were raised, the things they must have seen . . ." Peter paused, then shook his head before continuing. "Beatrice wasn't the only one in that family who was no stranger to violence."

Chapter
Eighteen

"That poor girl." Aunt Rose quickly stood up. "She's been through so much. I knew something was wrong, but I never imagined this. We must go see her."

Of course Rose would want to go to Cherise, I thought. Listening to people's problems, then counseling them to do the right thing, was what she and Peter both did so well.

I shot to my feet. Rose wasn't going anywhere without me. She already had her phone out and was scrolling through her contacts.

I grabbed my jacket and briefly considered calling Detective Sturgill. If I thought he would listen to me, I'd have informed him of this development. But I'd been in this position before, and I knew he would ask for proof.

Maybe after we talked to Cherise, Rose and I would be able to provide it.

Rose was holding her phone next to her ear and speaking into it in a low voice. A moment later, she disconnected the call and looked over at me. "Cherise is at her mother's house."

"What's she doing there?"

"She's working on getting the place packed up. She and Charlie intend to sell the house and they want to get it on the market as soon as possible."

It made sense that the siblings wouldn't want to hold on to a home that had been the scene of so many unhappy childhood memories—not to mention the location of their mother's tragic death.

"You're staying here," Rose said to Peter.

"Am I?" He lifted a brow. Unlike Rose and me, he hadn't risen from his seat. So perhaps he'd anticipated that.

"Yes." Rose had grabbed a heavy cardigan off the coatrack. She strode back to Peter and dropped a quick kiss on his forehead. "I'm depending on you to hold down the fort."

"Fort holding." He smiled. "One of my specialties."

"We won't be long," she told him. "And you needn't worry about a thing. If we run into any trouble, Melanie has that police detective's phone number on speed dial."

I do? That was news to me.

Aunt Rose was already out the door and on her way. I hurried to catch up. We hopped into the Volvo together.

"I suppose I had my suspicions . . ." Rose said as she fastened her seat belt.

I pulled out onto the road, then turned to look at her. "You did?"

She nodded.

"Why didn't you say something?"

"Because I hoped it wasn't true." She issued a heartfelt sigh. "Cherise's relationship with her mother has always been fraught with difficulties. The broken engagement was simply the last in a long line of arguments, where neither of them was willing to give an inch. When I heard that Cherise was the one who'd found Bea's body, I feared she might know more than she was letting on."

Yet another thing Rose had neglected to mention, I thought, annoyed. Hopefully, there wouldn't be more belated revelations to come.

"You should have told me," I said. "And you certainly should have shared your suspicions with Detective Sturgill."

"I couldn't do that. Think how horrible it would have been if I was wrong. Besides, I was a child of the sixties. My generation came of age with a healthy disrespect for authority."

Said the woman who'd spent her formative years in the convent, where the dictates of the Catholic Church and Mother Superior were law. Sometimes the disparate facets of my aunt's viewpoints gave me mental whiplash.

When Beatrice's house came into view, Rose turned to face me across the seat. "I'll go inside first. You may follow along behind—but quietly. Let me talk to Cherise. I don't want you upsetting her."

"Me?"

"Yes, you," she said firmly. "You can be quite stressful to have around, Melanie. And now we want everything to proceed smoothly. I'll let Cherise know she's in a safe place, and that she can tell me anything without fear of judgment."

"But—"

Rose tipped her head my way. Her expression silenced me.

"The important thing is for you to stay out of the way and let me do my job. I'm in charge of this operation. If you like, you may think of yourself as the muscle."

I bit my lip to keep from laughing. She'd been watching too many low-budget gangster movies. We weren't going to need any muscle. Aunt Rose and Cherise were simply going to have a civilized conversation—the contents of which I would later report to Detective Sturgill—while I apparently did my best to remain inconspicuous.

Easy, right?

Rose and I climbed the three steps leading to the front door together. Nudging me behind her, she pressed her finger firmly on the doorbell. We waited a minute in silence. Nothing happened.

I reached around her and rang the bell a second time. Above us, a second-story window was cracked open to let in some air. Music was playing inside the upstairs room. If Cherise was there, she probably couldn't hear us.

Rose frowned as I wrapped my fingers around the shiny brass doorknob. It turned easily and the door swung open. I gestured for her to precede me into the house.

"We can't just let ourselves in," she said.

"We can't just keep standing out here either."

Well, she could, but I wasn't about to.

I stepped past Rose into a spacious, two-story front hall. There was a round table with a bowl of flowers in front of me and a small chandelier hung overhead. The hardwood floor was polished to a high shine. But the feature that dominated the space was the grand, wraparound staircase that led to the home's second floor. There had to be nearly twenty stairs.

Involuntarily my eyes rose to the top, then followed its descent downward, ending on the unforgiving floor below. Of course, no sign of what had happened there remained. I swallowed heavily and made myself look away.

"I'll go first," Rose said. "Remember, you don't need to say a thing."

She shouldered me aside and marched up the wide staircase like a woman on a mission. Perhaps she, too, was recalling what had taken place where we now stepped. Her fingers traced a trail over the polished wooden banister as she advanced upward. I kept my hands to myself and followed behind.

The door at the top of the stairs was open, and the music grew louder as we approached. Cherise was in the room, standing beside a wide double bed. Its fringed pillows and damask duvet were barely visible beneath the piles of clothing that were scattered on top of it. Cherise was holding a silk blouse in her hands. Her head was turned away from us, her attention focused on something we couldn't yet see.

Then I stepped through the doorway and realized that she was looking at Charlie. I hadn't expected to find him here. Judging by the expression on his face, the surprise was mutual.

"What the hell?" Frowning, he reached over and turned down the music.

Cherise glanced our way. "Don't be difficult, Charlie. I told Rose she could come. She offered to help out."

"And I brought Melanie with me," Rose added brightly. "More hands make light work."

"We also want to talk to you about your

mother," I announced, then winced as Rose dug an elbow into my side.

Charlie was emptying the contents of an ornate armoire into a cardboard box. "What about her?"

"We know you were here the night she died," I said to Cherise. That was still a guess at this point—but the horrified expression on the woman's face told me everything I needed to know.

"That's a lie," Charlie growled. "You have no idea what you're talking about."

Rose hissed something under her breath.

I ignored everyone but Cherise. Her hands had gone still. The silk blouse she'd been folding slithered out of her fingers and landed in a heap on the bed.

"The two of you had another fight, didn't you?" I said. "Was this one about Scott too?"

Cherise lifted her chin, then glared at Rose. "No, it was about the shelter. That place is sponging up my mother's money like water—money I could be putting to much better use."

"Like getting your fiancé back?" I asked.

"We'd be planning our wedding right now if she hadn't gotten in the way," Cherise snapped.

Charlie strode across the room and grabbed his sister's arm. He pulled her around to face him. "You told me you weren't here that night. You said you didn't know anything about what happened before you found Mom the next morning."

Cherise stared into her brother's eyes. Her lower lip began to tremble. The woman was a better actress than I'd have guessed.

"I don't," she said quickly.

Except that she'd just said differently. And we'd all heard it.

Charlie nodded. Then he turned back to Rose and me. "My sister doesn't know what she's saying. She hasn't been herself lately. Obviously our mother's death was a huge shock to both of us. I think you'd better leave."

"I think you'd better listen to what your sister is telling you," I said. "She was here . . . in this house . . . when your mother fell. And she didn't do anything to help her."

I stopped short—deliberately—of accusing Cherise of engineering Beatrice's fall. If Charlie threw us out now, we might never find out what really happened.

"You're doing this to get back at me, aren't you?" he demanded. "You're angry because I intend to take back our parents' home."

"Don't be ridiculous," I said forcefully. "The fact that you've been acting like an ass has nothing to do with your sister's confession. Rose's shelter honors your mother's memory. Maybe you don't want to admit that, but you know it's true."

"What's true?" Charlie ground out.

"That your mother was a victim of domestic violence."

Rose whipped around and glared at me.

"What?" I said. "It's not as if they don't know. They both spent their childhoods living through it."

Cherise closed her eyes for several seconds, as if that could block out my words. When she spoke again, her face was damp with tears. "You have no idea what it was like."

"Of course we don't," Rose said gently. "But I'm here for you if you want to talk about it."

"Don't!" Charlie snapped.

Cherise yanked away from him. She folded her arms tightly over her chest. "Whenever we did something wrong, Mother would shake her fist at us. She told everyone she ruled her house with an iron fist. What a joke. Where was that iron fist when she needed it? She should have used it on our father."

"Cherise, stop it!" Charlie reached for his sister, but she dodged away.

"Stop what?" she cried. "Telling the truth? Finally admitting to the dirty little secret we've kept quiet about all these years? I'm done lying about it, Charlie."

"My sister is hysterical," he said to Rose and me. "Don't listen to her."

Cherise blinked away her tears and shook her head. Charlie was wrong. She wanted us to know.

She edged over to where Rose was standing.

"You understand. I know you do. You'll help me, won't you?"

"Of course I will." Rose slid an arm around the girl's trembling shoulders. "After all you've been through, you need someone on your side. Your mother's death was an accident, wasn't it?"

This time it was my turn to glare at Rose. *Don't put words in her mouth.*

Cherise's head lifted. Her expression brightened. She looked as if she'd just glimpsed a ray of light at the end of a very long tunnel.

"Yes, you're right. It was an accident." She looked at her brother. "It wasn't my fault. Mom stumbled and there was nothing I could do to save her."

Charlie's face had gone white. "Tell me you didn't do it, Cherise. Tell me right now."

"It was an accident," she repeated.

"Say the words," he ground out. "Say you didn't do it, or I will never forgive you."

Cherise began to cry again. Her body shook with huge, heaving sobs. "You're thinking that it should have been me, aren't you?" she accused. "You wish I was the one that fell."

Charlie opened his mouth as if to speak. Cherise bit her lip, watching, waiting for him to say something. When he didn't, her expression crumpled.

"Then this will make you happy," she said.

Cherise spun away from Rose and dashed toward the open doorway. We all stared after her in shock.

"Oh good Lord!" cried Rose. "She's not going to . . . ? Melanie, do something!"

I tried to grab her, but I wasn't fast enough. Cherise was already past me and out the bedroom door. The staircase was only a few steps away.

Thankfully Charlie was quicker. He caught up with his sister as she paused, quivering, at the top of the long stairway. Before she could take another step, he'd wrapped his arms around her and pulled her back.

Cherise's body shook as he pressed her against his chest. Charlie was shaking too. "It's going to be okay," he murmured. "We'll get through this together. Just like we did when we were kids. We'll hold each other's hands and close our eyes, and everything will be all right."

Epilogue

While Rose dealt with the siblings, I called Detective Sturgill.

Once he heard about our conversation with Cherise, he jumped into action. By the time the police got to the house, Charlie had already been in touch with the Gallagher family lawyer. Charlie and Cherise had been told to say nothing until the attorney arrived, and Charlie was doing his best to ensure that his sister complied with that advice.

In the meantime, Rose and I both gave individual statements to Detective Sturgill. When they'd been completed, he indicated that our

presence was superfluous and sent us on our
way. I dropped Rose off at the shelter and I went
home to my family. The matter of Beatrice Gallagher's death was now officially out of my
hands, which came as a relief.

Spring break was almost over. After the previous hectic week, I was finally free to concentrate
on the upcoming holiday. With just one more
day until Easter, I still had plenty left to do.

This was the last year Kevin would believe in
the Easter Bunny, so I wanted to make our
Easter celebration memorable. The supplies I'd
bought at the mall were tucked away in an upstairs closet, along with both the boys' Easter
baskets. I had coconut and cream eggs, chocolate coins, marshmallow chicks, and plenty of
jelly beans to pile on top of the crinkly green
grass. Kevin's basket would also have Legos and
Matchbox cars. Davey was getting a new pair of
earbuds and a gift card to iTunes. A big chocolate rabbit would be standing alongside each
basket.

I was looking forward to putting everything
together, but nothing could be done until
Davey and Kevin were in bed on Easter eve. Saturday afternoon, I let Sam entertain the boys
while I packed up the car and drove to the shelter with a trio of new Easter baskets, a big pile of
candy, and three dozen brightly colored eggs.

Rose was waiting for me when I arrived at the
Gallagher House. We piled the candy and bas-

kets on her kitchen table. The hard-boiled eggs went into her refrigerator. Then Rose and I spent an hour walking around the shelter and finding the best places for her to hide the eggs the next morning.

"Don't forget where you've put them," I told her. "And count to make sure they all get found. Otherwise you'll be very sorry in a week or two."

"I hadn't thought about that," Rose said with a sudden look of dismay. "Maybe I should make a map."

"Don't worry. If any eggs are still missing when the hunt is finished, I'll bring Bud over," I said with a smile. "That dog can sniff out something edible no matter where it is."

On my way out, Aunt Rose introduced me to the adorable, floppy-eared bunny who would serve as the prize for whichever child found the most Easter eggs. The rabbit sat up on his hind legs, nose twitching, as he peered at us from inside his wire cage. He was gray and white, with big dark eyes, and fur that was as soft as silk.

Thank goodness Kevin wasn't with me. That child would have fallen in love in a heartbeat.

"You're not going to give him away, right?" I said. Rose and I had gone over this before, but I wanted to be sure. "He's a living creature, and he needs a responsible adult to be in charge of his care."

"Yes, I know." She sighed. "Peg has been hounding me about that all week."

Good. If Aunt Peg was on the bunny's case, that meant I could relax. Rose might be tempted to ignore my instructions, but no one would dream of ignoring Aunt Peg.

Early the next morning, Sam and I put out Davey and Kevin's Easter baskets, then hid our colored eggs around the house. The Poodle pack followed us from room to room, observing our actions curiously. Bud was probably taking notes for future reference.

We finished getting everything set up just in time. It was barely light out when Kevin came flying down the stairs in his jammies. His eyes were shining with excitement as he raced into the dining room.

"The Easter Bunny came!" he squealed. "He filled my Easter basket and Davey's too, and he even left us an extra basket of dog biscuits."

"That Easter Bunny must be pretty smart," Davey said, coming down to join us. "He thought of everything."

"Can we have candy for breakfast?" Kevin was eyeing a row of yellow Peeps.

"Since it's Easter, you can each have one piece of candy now," Sam told him. "After that, we're going to hunt for eggs, and then I'm going to make a batch of my famous French toast."

Davey unwrapped a chocolate cream egg. I scooped up a handful of jelly beans. Kevin snatched a marshmallow chick and stuffed it in his mouth.

"I wish it was Easter every day," he said happily.

Davey snickered. "If it was, Mom would weigh twice as much."

"Hey!" I started to correct him, then shrugged instead. Sad to say, he was probably right.

Two days later, Aunt Rose called to thank me for my help. The Easter celebration at the shelter had been a resounding success, and the bunny was now named Fluffy. She also had some surprising news to divulge.

"You'll never guess what happened," she said. "Charlie came by this morning. He brought the deed to the Gallagher House with him. He'd signed it over to Peter and me."

"You're kidding."

"I would never joke about something like that," Rose replied primly.

"Do you think that means he was lying when he told you Beatrice had changed her mind about supporting the shelter?"

"That's one possibility," Rose allowed. "Another is that he's feeling guilty for having not realized just how toxic the relationship between Cherise and their mother had become. I think he may be trying to make reparations."

"Better late than never," I muttered.

Rose pretended not to hear me. "Charlie's motives aren't entirely altruistic, however. He's also asked us to join him in publicizing his generous donation. With Cherise's involvement in

Bea's death currently under investigation, Charlie hopes to sway the court of public opinion in their favor."

"That sounds more like what I'd expect of him."

Once again, Rose chose to ignore my comment. "There's one more possibility. Perhaps this is the Easter miracle Peter and I have been praying for. I'd like to think that this development is an affirmation that the work we're doing here has real value."

"Of course it does," I told her. "Any of the women who've found refuge at the Gallagher House could tell you that."

"I also have some other news to share." Suddenly I could hear the smile in Rose's voice. "Peter's latest round of testing has yielded excellent results. So it looks as though we have two Easter miracles to be thankful for."

"That's the best news of all," I said happily.

"Now that everything seems to be working out, life suddenly feels a little dull," she mused.

"I like dull," I said.

"No, you don't," Rose sniffed. "Nobody believes that. Put your thinking cap on, Melanie. What shall you and I get up to next?"

Dear Readers,

For years Melanie Travis has starred in her own mystery series, with Aunt Peg hovering—not altogether quietly—in the background. Eager to share her opinions and dispense advice, Peg has always grabbed center stage whenever she's had the chance. Now I'm delighted to announce that she'll have the opportunity to be totally in charge when she gets her own mystery to solve.

At long last, Peg will have everything her own way. Or will she?

Rose Donovan is Peg's sister-in-law. She's been a thorn in Peg's side for forty years. But somehow, when Rose decides to join a local bridge club, she can't think of anyone she'd rather have as her partner than Peg. Apart, these two women can be difficult. Together, they're more trouble than a sack of cats. Perhaps it's no surprise that when a member of the bridge club is murdered, Peg and Rose are named as suspects.

I had a great time writing *Peg and Rose Solve a Murder*, which is now available wherever print and e-books are sold. Peg has been a voice inside my head for so long that I loved being able to finally let her out to do her own thing. I hope you'll give her book a try. Otherwise Peg will never let you hear the end of it—and trust me, nobody wants that.

Happy reading!

Laurien

Chapter
One

Peg Turnbull was standing in the hot sun on a plot of hard-packed grass, staring at a row of Standard Poodles that was lined up along one side of her show ring. She'd been hired to judge a dozen breeds at the Rowayton Kennel Club Dog Show, and she couldn't imagine a better way to spend a clear summer day. Judging dogs involved three of her favorite things: telling people what to do; airing her own opinions; and of course, interacting with the dogs themselves.

A tall woman in her early seventies, Peg had a discerning eye and a wicked sense of humor. In this job she needed both. Aware that she'd be on her feet for most of the day, she had dressed that morning with comfort in mind. A cotton shirtwaist dress swirled around her legs. A broad brimmed straw hat shaded her face and neck. Her feet wore rubber-soled sneakers, size ten.

Though her career as a dog show judge had taken her around the world, today's show was local to her home in Greenwich, Connecticut. Peg had arrived at the showground early. She'd begun her assignment at nine o'clock with a selection of breeds from the Toy Group. Now, two and half hours later, she finally found herself facing her beloved Standard Poodles.

As she gazed at the beautifully coiffed entrants in front of her, Peg knew exactly what she was looking for—a sound, elegant, typey dog displaying the exuberant Poodle temperament. Having devoted her life to the betterment of the Poodle breed, and spent the previous decade judging numerous dog shows, Peg was well aware there were days when those coveted canine attributes could be in short supply. Thankfully, this first glimpse of her Open Dog class had already indicated that this wasn't going to be one of them.

Peg flexed her fingers happily. She couldn't wait to get her hands on the Poodles. She was eager to delve through their copious, hairsprayed coats to assess the muscle and structure that lay beneath. It was time to get to work.

A throat cleared behind her. "Peg?"

Marnie Clark was Peg's ring steward for the day. While Peg evaluated her entries and picked the winners and losers, it was Marnie's job to keep things running smoothly. That was no small feat. To the uninitiated, the arrangement of classes, record keeping, and points awarded could appear to rival a Rubik's Cube in complexity.

Marnie was an officer of the show-sponsoring kennel club. She was bright, vivacious, and two decades younger than Peg. Peg's Poodles and Marnie's Tibetan Terriers were both Non-Sporting Group breeds. The two women had known and competed against each other for years.

Reluctantly, Peg turned away from the four appealing Open dogs to see what Marnie wanted. The woman was holding up an unclaimed armband. The fifth Standard Poodle entered in the class had yet to arrive.

Absent? Peg wondered. *Or merely late?*

Each exhibitor was responsible for being at the ring on schedule. However, busy professional handlers with numerous breeds to show could sometimes find their presence required in more than one ring at the same time. In those cases, it was up to the judge to decide whether or not a concession would be made.

Peg glanced at the armband and lifted a brow.

Marnie wasn't supposed to tell her the missing exhibitor's name—a nod to impartiality that didn't fool anyone. The dog show world wasn't large. As soon as the handler arrived, Peg would recognize him or her, just as she knew the other exhibitors currently in her ring. As long as a judge remembered to evaluate the dogs on their merits and not their connections, that didn't have to be a problem.

Marnie obviously agreed. "It's Harvey," she said under her breath.

The steward nodded toward a big, black Poodle waiting just outside the gate with the handler's harried-looking assistant. Peg hadn't seen the young man before. He must be new. He was casting frantic glances toward the Lhasa Apso ring farther down the row of enclosures.

Peg took a quick look herself. Yes, indeed, there was Harvey—standing in the middle of a class of Lhasas that he very clearly wasn't winning. The handler was glaring at the indecisive judge as if he wanted to throttle her.

Peg felt much the same way. In her opinion, anyone who didn't want to have to make tough choices shouldn't apply for a judging license. Peg presided over her ring with the deft precision of a general inspecting troops. People might not agree with every decision she made, but they all respected her ability to get the job done.

Peg turned back to Marnie. "Give the young man the armband. Tell him to bring the dog in the ring and take him to the end of the line. You can switch Harvey in when he gets here."

"I already tried that," Marnie told her with a sidelong smirk. "The poor guy looked like he might faint. I wouldn't be surprised if this was his first dog show."

"And possibly his last." Peg felt an unwanted twinge of sympathy. It was no wonder that Harvey's assistants always looked stressed. The handler had entirely too many clients to do each one justice.

On the other hand, she was well aware that Harvey's Open dog was a handsome Standard Poodle who compared favorably with the others now in the ring. Unless she was mistaken, the dog only needed to win today's major to finish his championship. Harvey would be devastated if he missed this chance.

Peg sighed. Time was a valuable commodity for a dog show judge. And now hers was passing. She was done dithering.

"I'll start the class but take things slow," she said to Marnie. "Harvey has my permission to enter the ring when he gets here. But for pity's sake, do try to hurry him along."

Ten minutes later, Harvey made it to the ring in time, but only just. Peg leveled a beady-eyed glare in the handler's direction as he took possession of the big Poodle at the end of the line. Her meaning was clear to everyone in the vicinity. She'd granted Harvey leniency this time, but he shouldn't make a habit of needing it.

After weighing the merits and flaws of her

male Standard Poodle entry, Peg was further annoyed when her earlier speculation proved to
be true. She ended up awarding Harvey's dog
the title of Winners Dog and the coveted three
point major that went with it. With an outcome
like that, Harvey would never learn better manners. But darn it, the dog had deserved the win.
So what else was she supposed to do?

Peg hated it when her principles found themselves at odds with each other.

It didn't help that Marnie was laughing behind her hand as she called the Standard Puppy
Bitch class into the ring.

"Wait until you get approved to judge," Peg
said as they crossed paths at the judge's table.
"Then I'll come and make fun of you."

"As if you'd stoop to stewarding," Marnie
sniffed. Then winked. Stewarding was a difficult
and often thankless job and they both knew it.

The Standard Poodle bitch classes passed without incident. Peg took the time to reassure a ner-
vous novice handler whose lively puppy couldn't
keep all four feet on the ground. The woman left
the ring delighted with her red second-place ribbon in a class of just two.

In the Open class, Peg purposely paid scant
attention to a local handler who'd brought her
a black Standard bitch that wasn't at all her
type. The man had shown under Peg on many
previous occasions. He would have known that
she preferred a more refined Poodle, not to

mention one with a correct bite. He would also have been aware, however, that Peg and the Poodle's owner were friends.

No doubt he was hoping to capitalize on that relationship.

The implication made Peg steam. If the handler had the nerve to think that would sway her decision, he deserved the rebuke she was about to deliver. With a dismissive flick of her hand, Peg sent the pair to cool their heels at the back of the line. Then she awarded the class, and subsequently the purple Winners Bitch ribbon, to a charming apricot bitch she hadn't previously had the pleasure of judging.

After that, Best of Variety was an easy decision. It went to a gorgeous Standard who was currently the top winning Poodle on the East Coast. The apricot bitch was Best of Winners, which meant she shared the three-point major from the dog classes. Her elated owner-handler pumped Peg's hand energetically when she handed him his ribbon.

"You certainly made someone happy," Marnie commented as she turned the pages of her catalog to the next breed on the schedule.

"Yes, and my fingers may never recover." Peg smiled. "He was so excited by the win, I was afraid for a moment that he might burst into tears. Were we ever that young and enthusiastic?"

"Of course we were. It's just that it was so long

ago, we're too old to remember what it was like."

Peg turned away and surveyed her table. If Marnie was old, what did that make her? Perhaps it was better not to think about that.

She grabbed a sip of water from her bottle, then flipped her judge's book to a new page. Miniature Poodles were up next, and they'd drawn a big entry. Dogs and handlers were already beginning to gather outside the ring.

More fun coming right up.

"I wonder what that lady's story is," Marnie said. "Even in beautiful weather like this, dog shows hardly ever draw spectators anymore."

Not like in the good old days, Peg thought. She was arranging her ribbons and had yet to look up. "What lady?"

"Over there." Marnie gestured discreetly. "She's sat through four different breeds. There's a catalog in her lap but she looks like she hasn't the slightest idea how to read it."

"Maybe she just loves dogs," Peg said happily. *Welcome to the club.* She straightened to have a look, then abruptly went still. "Oh dear."

Marnie was heading to the in-gate. It was time to start handing out numbered armbands. She glanced back at Peg over her shoulder. "What?"

"That's my sister-in-law, Rose."

"Okay. Then that makes sense."

"Not to me," Peg muttered.

Chapter
Two

Peg finished her Mini Poodle judging by making the handsome white puppy her Best of Variety winner. Since she put the dog up over two finished champions, her selection caused some minor grumbling among the other exhibitors. Not that anyone would dare say anything to her face, of course.

"Don't worry," Marnie told her. The show photographer had been called to the ring so they could take pictures of the morning's winners before the lunch break. They were waiting for the man to appear. "I've got your back."

"Thank you," Peg replied. "I wasn't worried, however. Should I be?"

Marnie returned to her side. "She's really a relative of yours?"

Peg nodded.

"And you hadn't noticed she's been sitting there for an hour?"

"Apparently not." Why would she waste time perusing the ringside when she had all those lovely dogs in her ring?

"Right." Marnie didn't sound convinced.

Now that Marnie and Peg were both looking in her direction, Rose lifted a slender hand in a tentative wave. Her pleasant features were framed by a firm jaw and a cap of short gray hair was brushed back off her forehead. She was perched on the seat of a folding chair with her head up and her back straight. Rose had always had excellent posture.

Marnie smiled and waved back. Peg remained still.

Marnie gave Peg a little push. "Go say hello to her."

"I think not."

"Don't be silly. You have plenty of time."

Peg drew herself up to her full height. Even in sneakers, she neared six feet. "Not now. I have Minis to judge—"

"You're running early. I won't call the puppy dogs into the ring for at least two minutes."

"Rose can wait. I have a lunch break after Minis. She and I will talk then. Or maybe we won't." Peg pulled her gaze away. "Her choice."

"I see." Marnie bit her lip. It suddenly sounded as though this had ceased to be any of her business. "Then let me just finish handing out these armbands and we can get started."

Peg refused to let herself be distracted by her sister-in-law's presence as the first class of Miniature Poodle dogs filed into the ring. She had a job to do. Numerous exhibitors had honored her with an entry, and each of them deserved her complete attention.

Still, it was hard not to sneak a peek in Rose's direction every so often. What on earth was she doing here? As far as Peg knew, Rose didn't like dogs. Nor did she like Peg.

That feeling was mutual.

Animosity had sizzled between the two women since Peg became engaged to her beloved, and now dearly departed husband, Max, more than four decades earlier. In all the intervening years, neither Rose nor Peg had managed to put the things that were said during that rocky time entirely behind them. Max was Rose's older brother—and a man for whom Peg would have done anything. Yet even he had never succeeded in forging a friendship between the two most important women in his life.

Peg plucked a stunning white youngster from the Puppy class and awarded him the points over the older dogs. She suspected once she'd seen the rest of her Mini entry, he would win Best of Variety too. That would be a bold move

on her part. People would ta
was bound to be talk.

As she waited for the first bit
ring, Peg allowed herself a sma
faction. The white puppy was a s
ing. He would finish his champio
and she would be known as the ju
covered him.

Buoyed by the prospect of that su
lowed her gaze to flicker briefly in F
tion. It aggravated Peg that she felt
to gauge her sister-in-law's reaction.
vated her even more than to see that
none.

Rose had set aside her catalog. I
hands were folded demurely in her lap.
pression was bland, her features arrang
mask of resigned complacency that P
infuriatingly well.

Of course Rose hadn't noticed any
usual. She probably couldn't tell the
between a Miniature Poodle and a ha

That brought Peg back to her earli

It was never good news when Rose
Peg wondered what the woman wan

"You didn't hear what Dan Fogel said as he left the ring."

Fogel was a busy and successful professional handler with a very high opinion of himself and his dogs. He clearly hadn't been pleased when Peg moved the white puppy up from the middle of the line and placed it in front of his specials dog.

"And I don't want to either," Peg said firmly. "Considering all the breeds he handles, Dan shows under me frequently. If a momentary lapse in judgment caused him to say something unfortunate, I'm better off not knowing about it. I'd hate for it to taint my opinion of him in the future."

"Your loss. He used some rather colorful language." Marnie grinned. "For what it's worth, I'd have done the same thing you did. There wasn't a better moving dog in the variety ring than that puppy."

Once the photographer arrived, a dozen pictures were taken in quick succession. Everybody knew the drill. Pose the dog, hold up the ribbon, smile, flash! Done, and on to the next.

"Lunchtime," Marnie said happily when they were finished. "I can't wait to get off my feet for a few minutes."

"You go ahead." Peg glanced toward the side of the ring. "I'll catch up."

Apparently the extra time Peg had spent tak-

ing photographs had been the last straw for
Rose. Now she was squirming in her seat. Peg
didn't blame her. Those folding chairs weren't
meant for long-term use.

"Sounds good." Marnie followed the direction of Peg's gaze. "I'll save you a place."

The two women exited the show ring together. Marnie headed toward the hospitality
tent. Peg went the other way, striding around
the low, slatted barrier that formed the sides of
the enclosure. She stopped in front of Rose,
who looked up and smiled.

"Good morning, Peg."

"Afternoon, now," Peg replied smartly. There
was another chair nearby. She dragged it over
and sat down. "Imagine my surprise to find you
sitting outside my ring. What are you doing
here?"

"I was curious. I came to see what you do for a
living."

Peg wasn't buying that for a moment. But she
was willing to play along. "And?"

"It's rather boring, isn't it?"

"Not to me." Peg's smile had a wolflike quality, more a matter of bared teeth than shared
humor.

"Perhaps not. I'm sure you know more about
these things than I do."

Having been immersed in the sport of pure-
bred dogs for the majority of her adult life, Peg
knew more about *these things* than ninety-nine

percent of the world's population. She might have been tempted to point that out except it sounded as though Rose was trying to be agreeable. And that immediately made Peg suspicious.

"If you found the judging boring, why did you stay?" she asked pleasantly.

Rose shifted sideways in her seat. Now she and Peg were face-to-face.

"I think it's time you and I got to know each other better."

Peg's mouth opened. Then closed. She could have sworn she already knew more about Rose than any sane person would ever want to know.

"Why would we want to do that?"

"Because despite our differences, we're family."

Family. Huh. As if that was a good excuse.

Peg's eyes narrowed. "What are you up to?"

"What do you mean?" Rose's reply was all innocence.

Abruptly, Peg was reminded that her sister-in-law had found a vocation early in life. She'd entered the convent straight out of high school and spent most of the intervening years as Sister Anne Marie of the Order of Divine Mercy. Rose had perfected that serenely guileless look during her time in the convent. She still used it to great effect on occasion.

Peg wasn't fooled. Having been called both a heathen and a sinner by Rose in the past, she disdainfully thought of the expression as Rose's *nun face.*

"As entertaining as it is to spar with you," she said, "I'm sure you can see that I'm quite busy today. If you have something to say to me, please do so. If not, it's time for my lunch."

The other woman sighed heavily. That was Peg's cue to stand up. Somewhere on the showgrounds there was a rubbery prewrapped sandwich calling her name. And a trip to the porta-potty wouldn't go amiss either.

"Wait," Rose said. "Give me a minute."

"I've already given you three."

"Sit back down. Please?"

It was the novelty of hearing the word *please* that did it. Peg thought that might be the first time she'd ever heard Rose voice such an appeal. She swished the skirt of her shirtwaist dress to one side and sat.

"Go on," she said.

"I want to join a bridge club. And I want you to join with me as my partner."

"You're joking."

"No." Rose frowned. "Why would I joke about something like that?"

"Because it's funny?"

It was funny, wasn't it? Any moment now, the two of them would dissolve into laughter. Not that they'd ever done so before. Belatedly it occurred to Peg that it didn't appear to be happening this time either.

Instead, Rose was simply sitting there, staring at her. Her calm manner was almost unnerving.

"A bridge club," Peg repeated. Apparently it wasn't a joke. "I would think you'd be too busy for a frivolous pastime like that."

"Of course I'm busy. But I can't spend all my time doing good works." Rose managed to deliver that statement with a straight face. "Besides, bridge isn't a frivolous game. You should know that. You used to play."

Yes, she had. But how did Rose know that?

"You mentioned it once." Rose answered the unspoken question. "You were talking about living in a dorm when you were in college. You said every night after dinner, you and your friends would go down to the living room for demitasse and bridge."

Peg was slightly stunned. "That was fifty years ago."

"Even so. You talked about it."

Peg shook her head. She barely remembered playing bridge, much less having a conversation about it later. And with Rose of all people. How had that come about? She had no idea.

"I never went to college," Rose said in a small voice.

"No. You left home to become a nun instead."

"I had a vocation."

Even Peg wasn't mean enough to point out that Rose's vocation had apparently vanished like a puff of smoke when—after more than three decades in the convent—she had met a priest and fallen in love. Peter and Rose had recently celebrated their tenth wedding anniversary, however. So there was that.

"I realize now that there are many things I missed out on in my youth," Rose said.

"That was your choice," Peg pointed out.

"I didn't know that then. I was young enough and naive enough to think that God had made the choice for me. Now that I'm older, I realize that there are many paths to eternal salvation."

"And one of them includes playing bridge?" Peg regretted the words as soon as they'd left her mouth. In all the years she and Rose had known each other, they'd never had a conversation quite like this. All at once, Peg didn't want to be the one responsible for shutting it down. "I'm sorry. That was uncalled for."

"No, I get it. You're skeptical. I probably deserve that."

"Yes, you do."

"That goes both ways."

Peg snorted. "Don't tell me you're waiting for an apology."

"Of course not." A small smile played around the corners of Rose's mouth. "I know better than that. But I didn't come here today to fight with you."

After a pause, Peg shrugged. "It wasn't on my calendar either."

The two women shared a look of mild accord.

It wasn't quite rapprochement, but perhaps a small step in that direction.

"I gather you're missing lunch on my account," Rose said. "I passed a food concession on my way in. Maybe I could buy you a salad?"

Peg nearly laughed. "Thank you, but no. Obviously you've never had dog show food."

"That bad?"

"Probably even worse than you're imagining."

"All right, then." Rose reached down into a canvas tote beside her chair and pulled out a shiny red orb. "Apple?"

Peg accepted the piece of fruit. She studied the apple from all angles, then took her first bite. "Maybe you should tell me something about your bridge club. I haven't played the game in years. I may not be up to their standards." She cocked a brow in Rose's direction. "Or yours."

"You don't have to worry about that. My friend, Carrie, belongs to the group. From what she's told me, the members enjoy getting together to play bridge, but they aren't seriously dedicated to the game. They don't play duplicate or anything like that. Just plain old rubber bridge, and it's mostly for fun and socializing."

"What about Peter?" Peg asked. "I would think you'd want to play with him."

"His game is chess, not bridge," Rose told her. "Besides, just because he and I are married doesn't mean we have to do everything together."

Peg helped herself to another bite of the apple and stared off into the distance. She and Max had done everything together. Their relationship had been one of moving in tandem toward shared goals and accomplishments. They'd created a family of renowned Standard Poodles, while building a life that suited each of them perfectly. Max had been the other half of Peg's whole. Even a decade after his death, she still felt incomplete without him. Peg would have given anything to have those days to live over again.

"Plus, I like to win," Rose was saying. "So I'd prefer to have a partner who's competitive. Someone cutthroat like you."

Peg blinked, yanking her thoughts back to the present. "Cutthroat?"

"You know what I mean. You make Genghis Khan look like a sissy."

Peg suspected she was meant to be offended. In truth, she didn't mind the comparison. Strength was a virtue in her eyes. Speaking of which, Rose wasn't giving in and going away like she usually did whenever the two of them crossed paths. Maybe she possessed more backbone than Peg knew about.

"Apparently you're not as mild-mannered as you'd like people to believe," she said.

"Then perhaps we'd make a good team."

"We'd probably end up fighting with one another."

Rose shrugged. "We fight now, so what's the difference? Who knows? Maybe after all these years, we could become friends."

Peg nearly choked on her last bite of the apple. "I highly doubt that."

"Now you sound like a quitter."

"I do *not.*"

"A coward, then?"

"I see what you're doing," Peg said mildly. "You think if you back me into a corner, I will give you what you want."

"Not at all," Rose replied. "It seems to me this should be something we both want."

"How do you figure that?"

"Neither of us is getting any younger."

"So?"

"At our ages, life is all about personal connections. It's inevitable that we'll start losing people from our lives. Doesn't that make it even more important to appreciate the friends and family we have with us?"

Family. This was the second time Rose had referenced that relationship. As if things were really that simple. Unfortunately, where the Turnbull family was concerned, complications had always been a way of life.

Peg's heart squeezed painfully in her chest.

Rose did have a point about losing loved ones, however. Peg hadn't needed to reach the age of seventy-two before realizing that.

Still, she hated having to admit that Rose might be right about something. So instead she said, "I'll think about your offer and get back to you."

"Don't wait too long." Rose picked up her tote and stood. "This isn't an open-ended invitation. If you dawdle, I might find someone better."

Someone better. Peg blew out a breath. *Right.* Like that was going to happen.

Visit our website at
KensingtonBooks.com
to sign up for our newsletters, read
more from your favorite authors, see
books by series, view reading group
guides, and more!

BOOK ||||/|| CLUB
BETWEEN THE CHAPTERS

Become a Part of Our
Between the Chapters Book Club
Community and Join the Conversation

Betweenthechapters.net